Belle of the West

A. Henry Keene

I dedicate this work on 1 April 2015 to my loving wife, whose support made it possible.

A project such as this is truly a group effort, so I'd like to thank the many people who have contributed to its completion. In particular, I'd like to thank Brenda Lanham, Jerry Stephens, Cindy Stephens, James Ward Kirk, Krista Grabowski, Roger Cowin, Dale Hollin, Bob and Sally Lanham, Ethan Smith, Charles Breslin, Jay Kloner, Peggy Yurt, Lauri Adkins, and Marty Edlin.

Note on the first edition:

"Belle of the West" is a work in progress. Without full awareness, I've been working on it for the past three or four years. I release it now as a gift to my father. He is 81 and wants to hold it in his hands. I will continue to work on the project and update it with new editions as appropriate. Much work remains, and I have much to learn but shall not despair, since a lifetime of learning and writing lay ahead of me.

Thanks for your support.
A. Henry Keene
1 May 2015

Table of Contents

Meridiana

1

Andy runs a hand across his beard and chews his lower lip. *I must see Doc Laurent.* He slides the metal door along its overhead track, and the iron wheels rumble along the rail, until the grey metal slab slams shut to fill the alley with a clamorous thud. *Where did I last see Doc?* Andy squints and tries to remember but recalls only the vaguest impressions of a black-haired man. He checks his watch. Seven. *Carol is waiting for me at the Lowell gallery. Opening night. My show. First things first.*

It would have been a short walk to the left to the Lowell on the corner, but Andy walks to the right. He walks past large green dumpsters to the end of the dark, mist-filled alley, reaches the corner and turns right to see the Osiris building; Louisville's first postmodern skyscraper rises from the fog to loom over the iron facades and arched windows from the city's bustling river port days. Its pyramid glows atop the architectural mishmash of future and past along with moon-bright clouds in the black sky.

He walks the crumbling sidewalk and cobblestone side streets, wanders down graffiti-filled alleys, strolls past piss-soaked drunks and scurrying rats. Left and right and round and round, Andy ambles aimlessly. Then he rounds the corner onto Main Street, and the distant glow of an old-fashioned neon sign fills his vision. He focuses on the eerie light and walks toward it. As he nears the sign, he makes out the image depicted by the bright lights, and a sense of recognition comforts him. It is a southern gentleman, complete with hat, thin bowtie and pointed goatee.

Approaching the sign, Andy feels an inexplicable giddiness and smiles. The last hour of wandering has lead him to the neon Colonel, and he feels like a pilgrim reaching Mecca or a Buddhist attaining emptiness. Somehow, he knows this is his destination and walks briskly toward the sign until he sees, beneath it, a doorkeeper, motionless, staring, scowling. Andy's pace slows, as his legs and back and neck stiffen. When he gets to within five feet of the man, Andy sees his tattoo. A three-headed dog. Andy stops. He stares at the image, imagines the dogs growling and showing their sharp teeth. He looks back across his shoulder, considers turning back, but decides to press on. He must know the Colonel's secret.

He draws a quivering breath and wills his feet to move. His arms shiver a bit and the corners of his mouth draw back, and just as Andy comes within arm's length the doorkeeper turns to face him. Andy feels the pressure of his direct gaze. His heart throbs, his leg stiffens, and his toe scuffs the sidewalk. Andy blushes deep red, and, behind him, the doorkeeper smiles a bit.

Walking stiffly, Andy reaches the corner and stops before a large window with light streaming through it. He settles before the plate glass, stands in the white fog and peers into the gallery to study the large paintings inside. His eyes shift from canvas to canvas, skips from image to image.

"Where have you been?" Carol's voice expresses concern and consternation. Her eyebrows knit together, as she tilts her head to look into his unresponsive eyes. "Andy?" Her soft features and wavy brown hair glow in the chiaroscuro lighting, as she slowly approaches and puts her hand on his shoulder. "Andy." She shakes him gently. "Wake up."

He becomes aware of the beating of his heart and warmth at the core of his chest. His fingertips tingle. A surge of viscous warmth creeps through his torso and the hairs on his head stand slightly. He gasps and blinks.

Carol notices his dilated pupils and takes his hand. "Can you do this? The opening?" Carol sighs. "Can you do it?"

"I guess." He feels her embrace him and press her palm gently against his cheek. He closes his eyes to focus on the sensation of her warmth flowing into him. As he gradually regains his bearing and begins to focus on the world around him, a man wearing a tuxedo steps through the door. "Guest of honor arrives late to his own party." The man laughs, adjusts his black bowtie, and runs a palm along his neatly-combed hair to press down strays.

Andy looks at the man. "Hello, Daniel."

In the gallery, several of Louisville's well-dressed, well-heeled and well-known swirl wine in their glasses and chat among the paintings.

"That's Lester Jones." A man whispers to his wife. "He was head of Osiris healthcare until it sank a few years back, but he didn't go down with the ship. That scoundrel sold off his stock at the first sign of trouble, caused the whole thing to collapse and made a bundle."

Lester stands tall before a large, densely-decorated painting. He gazes at the broken patterns of tans and browns over a sooty background of misty greys until his eyes come to rest on a faceless female figure in the midst of the rush and swirl of color.

"It's her, Helen." Lester glances toward his wife and whispers, "Meridiana." He smiles. "Same hair. Same pose. Same erotic essence." He gestures toward the nude figure laying gracefully back in a pose expressing the perfect balance of elegance and debauchery.

Helen recognizes the name. She recalls Lester groaning it out in the midst of one of their sordid, sloppy, dream-time trysts. She knows Lester's plans for her, but this is the first time she has seen her image in all its seductive glory. Helen, a raven-haired beauty by any standard, is impressed with Meridiana's refined sexuality.

"She is so real, Helen. More real than in my dreams." He strokes Helen's arm. "I can almost see her breathe."

Helen isn't jealous of Meridiana. Every man has his fantasy, and, for Lester, she is the ideal woman: beautiful, elegant, and powerfully seductive. But Helen knows she is more than a fantasy, and this painting proves she is real. How else could a total stranger paint Lester's dream woman? No doubt, she exists in some realm. Helen looks at the painting to notice the individual hairs and the plumpness of her flesh. She feels Meridiana's presence as though the painting were not merely an image but an occult mirror, revealing the image while withholding the essence or being.

Staring at the painting, Lester imagines the painting hanging on the wall of his trophy room between deer heads and other animal skulls and artifacts. This will have to do until I can hold her in my arms, feel her supple flesh, smell her scent and sink deep into her welcoming embrace.

Helen focuses beyond the window, where the young couple embraces, and Daniel, the gallery owner and art dealer, talks with them. She watches Daniel tug the man's arm to separate the couple and feels as though she is watching someone wrest an infant from the bosom of its loving mother. Her mind is rapt with curiosity and concern, as Daniel leads the handsome young man to the doorway and his companion follows closely behind.

The trio enters the gallery, and Helen notices the young man's untidy brown hair and beard, framing his oval face. She sees his eyes, bluebird bright, and slides her palms down her waist and hips to smooth the sleek satin of her dress. Daniel looks her way, and Helen notices a slight smile on his lips as he leads the couple toward her and Lester.

They are intercepted by Leslie Flint, critic-at-large. She peers at Andy over her glasses, perched half-way down the bridge of her nose. "Oh, tell me, Daniel, is this the artist? Andy Leon? Pleased to meet you." She extends her hand. "Leslie Flint."

"Hello." Andy takes Leslie's hand.

"I gather your methods are surrealist and your mythos is Jungian. I detect hints of Klimt in both style and iconography and the strong influence of…"

As Leslie continues, Andy rubs his fingers against his palms.

"…and the existentialist sense of--"

"Good for you." Andy interrupts.

"You'll have to excuse him." Daniel slips his arm around Andy's shoulder. "He's a bit under the weather."

"Of course." She laughs.

"Come on." Daniel pulls Andy to himself. "Let's get you a glass of wine."

"I've got to see Doc Laurent." He looks into Daniel's eyes.

Daniel quickly looks around the gallery and smiles. "We'll talk later."

"Well, my dear," Leslie takes Carol by the elbow, "quite the catch you have there."

"Yes. He's—"

"Quite the talker."

"A tender soul."

"Very talented. But do you see his purpose?" Leslie studies Carol. "His goal?"

"He makes beautiful pictures." Carol swallows hard.

"Sweet girl." Leslie studies her own freshly-manicured nails. "He is attempting to manifest the imaginary. He is attempting to make reality." She smiles. "And he just may succeed."

Befuddled, Carol bites her lip. This talk of manifestation is so arcane, and the personage before her is so opaque and impenetrable. What's all the fuss is about? They're just pretty pictures. She looks about for Andy and sees Lester Jones, talking with Daniel. "The boy is on the verge. He is in touch with her." Then she sees Andy alone at the back of the gallery.

"Excuse me."

"Of course." Leslie smiles behind Carol, who rushes to Andy. She draws close to him, puts her hand on his cheek and searches his eyes. "Are you okay, baby?"

Andy shrugs.

"Let's get outta here." She looks about the gallery and sees a strangely-leering, white-haired man. "These people freak me out."

Andy's studio is a large former industrial space now filled with paintings, sculptures and found items. In one corner, a rusty car fender leans. In another corner stands an antique, velvet-covered chair. Stacked and leaning everywhere are the paintings, each displaying a different color and design, but all explore the same subject: a mysterious nude of unknown origin and indistinct facial features. Abstract and sketchy backgrounds give little or no indication of time or place, so the nude reigns as luring siren in a timeless, placeless realm.

The large metal door slides open to reveal Andy and Carol. They step across the threshold, and he slides the door closed. She walks to an open kitchen area at the back of the studio to make tea. He takes a deep breath, lets it slip out between barely-parted lips, and crosses the studio to collapse onto the velvet chair, which creaks as it receives his weight. He stretches his legs out, slumps deeply and props his chin up with a fist. Relaxing, he lets his mind settle into the comforting environment of familiar objects and habitual thoughts.

He contemplates the painting on an easel before him. It is a black rectangle, spotted with bright yellow bursts and vague indications of a city skyline. There, among the hints of setting, emerges the merest beginnings of a form: the legs of a woman curl beneath her bottom, and her torso twists so the figure faces away from the viewer, from Andy, who stares at the canvas. Pressure builds behind his eyes. His lips compress, and he sinks deeper into the corner chair. Will I ever be able to make her real? Give her the life and spirit she has in my dreams and visions? This is but the shadow of her actual being. Nothing but a pale imitation. I want to paint her into existence, to stand before the painting and feel myself in her intoxicating presence.

The teapot whistles. Andy continues staring. Carol pours hot water over the teabag into Andy's favorite blue cup and puts the cup on a yellow saucer. She walks to Andy and kneels by his side. When she sees the painting, discerns the graceful curves of the woman's body, she clamps her teeth tightly. Her face flushes. She glances at Andy, engrossed in his study of the woman. He loves her. She had not realized it before, but she sees now that he is obsessed, and there is nothing she can do about it. A chill runs through her body, and Carol becomes aware of the cold. She rubs her hands together, and, turning to Andy, kisses him on the forehead.

Carol rises to her feet and walks to their bed in the center of the studio. She gets on it and covers herself with several thick blankets.

It was the fall of 1984, Carol's sophomore year at the Christian Academy. She sat next to her best friend, Pam. The two had attended the school and had been best friends since kindergarten, but events of this day would drive between them a wedge, which would separate them from each other and their innocence.

Carol and Pam were jabbering about school when Andy entered the classroom like one destined to conquer it. Quietly and with an economy of motion, he strode through the door and stood. Something about him was unique. It was in his bearing: a certain casual aloofness. He looked past people, didn't pause to acknowledge them but kept his gaze moving. The students stared at him, and he looked about the room as though seeking the spot where, in the future, his marble bust would sit.

Nervous energy flowed through Carol's body, and she squirmed in her seat. Her face blushed, as she stared at the stranger. She felt Pam tug her arm, and the two shared gleeful expressions. When Andy's gaze swept her way, Carol saw Pam wave with her fingers and Andy's eyes shift to her. A smile flashed across his face, and he spotted the empty desk in front of Pam. Carol felt the sting of jealousy. He had seen Pam first. He had smiled at Pam first. Carol's heart thumped, as a wave of anger swept through her body. She watched Andy stroll down the aisle toward Pam, and she set a firm resolve to claim him. When Andy reached the desk, Carol caught his eye and slowly licked her lips. Andy stumbled, and knew she had succeeded.

In the fall of 1986, Carol and Andy attended the senior bonfire at the country home of one of the Academy's teachers.

Sitting with Carol by the crackling fire, Andy felt, for the first time, more than curiosity about her. He felt absolute desire. It began in his cells, reverberated through his bones and burned in his muscles.

"Let's walk around the lake." Andy tugged her hand. "Check out the boathouse."

They walked the short distance from the fire to the boathouse. Andy laid out his jacket and motioned for Carol to sit. When she did, Andy settled down next to her and leaned in to kiss her gently. It was the kind of tender gesture one expects from young lovers. Tentative and sweet, that first exploration of sensual delight set in motion the rising moon of sexual desire, whose gravitational pull brought to the surface of Andy's calm demeanor a fierce insistence, which soon overwhelmed his polite upbringing.

She shared the experience with no one, but from that moment formed a deep commitment to Andy and vowed to spend the rest of her life with him.

After high school, Carol and Andy moved into a small, makeshift studio. He spent his days painting and worked evenings at the grocery. She waited tables at the diner. They weren't getting rich, but Andy was pursuing his dream. That's what mattered.

When they were together, they enjoyed each other. They laughed a lot and made love regularly. It wasn't the most passionate sex, but Carol let him have his way with her. She wasn't especially lusty, didn't long for him in that way, but she grunted and moaned for his benefit, as he did what he had to do.

Perhaps she had promised more than she could deliver when she licked her lips back in school. Perhaps she had led him on, but she took care of him and wanted nothing more than to be near him. Why couldn't he be satisfied? Why couldn't he settle into the comfort of her loving embrace? Why had that whore invaded his dreams like an ancient army laying siege to some vulnerable citadel?

Andy throws back the big latch and heaves the door. It slides open to reveal Daniel along with Lester and Helen Jones in the alley.

"Daniel?" Andy rubs his face.

"I didn't get to introduce you to the Joneses." He smiles. "This is Lester and Helen."

"What the hell, Daniel? Can't you see we're sleeping?"

"It's noon."

"Still—"

"We won't be a minute." Daniel steps through the doorway. "We have business to discuss. A proposition."

Daniel slides the studio door shut, and the three neatly-dressed visitors stand in the disorderly space of the studio.

Carol, wrapped in an old blanket, stands across from Helen Jones. She notices the woman's black hair, flowing from beneath a soft cloche and ventures to look into her eyes. Helen's brilliant blue eyes, set in a symmetrical face, effortlessly return Carol's skittering gaze. Carol's body tenses, and she lowers her head slightly, allowing hair to fall across her face. "Tea?" She pulls the blanket tight around herself.

"Please."

Carol slouches toward the kitchen.

"Mind if we look around?" Daniel grasps Andy by the shoulder.

Andy exhales forcefully. "Help yourselves."

Daniel and Lester begin walking about the studio to look at the paintings.

Helen unbuttons her full length coat. "Do you mind?" She turns to Andy, who grasps the coat by the shoulders and lowers it to reveal her corseted waist and round bottom in a perfectly-fitted, red dress. His heartbeat turns jazzy, and he draws a long breath to calm himself.

Helen walks slowly toward the canvas in the corner, and Andy, holding her coat, follows.

"This one. You must tell me about it." She gestures gently toward Andy's current work and leans a bit, exposing her cleavage to him.

"Well," he swallows hard, "it's like the others."

"All the same?"

"Not the same." Andy struggles. "Just not so different."

"The woman." Helen smiles. "Tell me about her."

Andy watches her full lips move across the moist, round edges of her teeth as she talks.

"Someone you know?" She smiles. "Someone you'd like to know?"

Helen's voice tingles through his body.

"Fifty thousand dollars." Lester pronounces the words distinctly and takes a sip of his tea.

Carol clutches Andy's arm.

"That's a lot." Andy runs a hand through his hair.

"I have seen where your work is going, and I want you to succeed." Lester nods. "I will give you fifty thousand for your next painting, but it must fully realize the figure. I want to see her face and feel her warmth."

Andy notices Helen from the corner of his eye, secretly scans her round hips and narrow, corseted waist. He sniffs the air discretely. There's her scent: succulent, rich and moist like good garden soil ripe for tillage.

"Who are these people, Andy?"

"Rich assholes, I guess."

"I mean, really. Who does that? A six month stipend? Fifty thousand for a painting he hasn't even seen? And that wife of his. What a tart. I saw her flirting with you."

"That's just how they are, these people."

"Still. I want to know about them."

"What's important is that I could continue my work without worrying about the next sale. You could quit waiting tables. It's all good." Andy sips from his tea.

"And what is the deal with that key he gave you?"

"I don't know. I'm curious." Andy pulls the key from his pocket and looks at it. He notices the letters K.G.C. engraved on it. "He said to meet him at the club to let him know my decision. I think I know where it is." Andy nods. "A place on Main, just down from the Lowell, near the Osiris tower. Been by there a few times. Got a bouncer out front. Face like a pit bull." Andy shudders. "I'll check it out."

"Maybe." Carol licks her lips. "Maybe we can finally get married."

Andy's shoulders tighten. "I'd have to finish the painting first." Andy rubs the back of his neck. "Don't know if I can."

"Sure you can."

The two fall silent. They sink into the stillness of the studio, and Carol's heart aches with conflict. Fear and hope rise in her, and images of the faceless woman taunt her. Carol stirs her tea. The spoon tings against the cup, and Andy feels himself slipping away as he often does. The world grows distant and hazy. He raises a hand to his face to press his fingertips gently into the soft flesh of his cheek and feels it give. Within his body, something shrinks back, withdraws and compresses into a super-dense singularity, a glowing orb at the core of his being. In an instant, as though with the snap of a finger, it vanishes and he walks slowly toward the canvas in the corner.

Helen Jones was born Mary Helen Hornback. She was the only child of Catholic parents, who sacrificed everything to get their lovely girl the best education possible. She attended the best Catholic schools in Louisville and ended her education by going away to finishing school, where strict marms polished her with ever-finer manners and tastes. Upon her return to Louisville, she found only boredom and the mindless routine of family meals, polite conversation and tea on the porch. Gradually, she grew numb and disinterested. On the verge of depression, she wandered astray at the beckoning of a dark stranger.

It was the summer of ninety-nine. Helen sat on the front porch of her family's Audubon Park home. She sipped tea from a blue cup and listened to the mockingbirds, as the sun settled toward the horizon. Then she heard a distant rumble and felt her heart stutter. The rumble intensified as did the beating of her heart. Heat spread through her chest into her face, as a fierce, blue Chevelle crept round the corner. Her body vibrated in sympathy with the rumbling exhaust, as the gleaming car prowled past. Then she saw him, left arm hanging out the window, black hair slicked back. She was swept up in a whirlwind of rumbling masculinity, taken in by this show, entranced and enthralled by rolling thunder and mechanical menace.

From that moment, Helen spent her evenings awaiting the distant rumble and the slow passing of the mysterious outsider. He had become the focus of her dreams and fantasies of letting all her refinement and pretense go in an act of total submission. Then one evening, in anticipation of his arrival, she walked down the street to the small park, where she watched and waited.

As day turned to night, Helen felt the exciting rumble, and the sparkling Chevelle eased up a short distance from her. As the earth vibrated beneath her feet, she forced a deep breath and smelled the tangy, pungent gasoline vapor in the exhaust, tasted it, bitter and foul on her tongue. She cleared her throat and gasped another breath of the toxic fumes. Relentlessly, the engine rumbled, and she noticed the small ticking sounds of the valves and the whirring of belts. She heard and felt each cylinder fire its charge of compressed gasoline vapor in a precisely-timed series of explosions. She wanted to go to him, but her feet refused. She saw his muscular arm covered with prison tats and noticed an eye set within a dark triangle. Helen stared at the eye, felt it return her gaze in a sort of infinite feedback loop. She sighed, and her body relaxed deeply.

He raised his hand to point to the passenger door.

She moved a foot, hesitantly approached.

"Get in."

"What's--" Helen swallowed. "What's your name?"

"I'm Doc."

Doc entered the room at the Clark Motel. Helen followed him into the rust and brown room. She saw the bed, carelessly made up with a polyester spread and lumped up pillows, sitting catawampus.

She imagined stripping for Doc, slowly revealing her sumptuous curves and smooth flesh to him. He would breathe heavily and grow erect. She would lay back for him, spread herself on that hideously-stained, floral-print, polyester monstrosity. He would gaze at her, and his body would have no choice but to want her.

"I'd like to see your hair." Doc said smoothly. "Take off your hat."

She smiled a bit and blushed. Then she raised a hand to smooth her hair against her neck and reached for the brim of her hat.

With a mellow voice, Doc said, "That's it. Just toss it anywhere."

When Helen pulled the hat from her head and dropped it to the floor, Doc smiled. This job will be easy.

"Have a seat. Make yourself comfortable. I'm not going to hurt you."

He noticed her breathing slow and said, "Breathe slow and deep."

Helen took a deep breath. When she let it out, her shoulders fell and she blinked slowly.

"Now you are relaxed, and you feel the warmth of your body."

Helen felt a swirling wave of molten energy in her chest. It flowed through her neck, which loosened. She felt the warmth in her face, and her cheeks flushed. She relaxed, settled into the chair, and let her eyelids droop slightly.

"Your eyelids are growing heavy."

Helen felt them slide down to obscure her vision. She struggled to open them a bit and made out Doc's form, a dark silhouette.

"They are sooo heavy, and you are sooo warm."

Her eyes fell closed.

"That's it. Just relax into a deeeeep, deeeeep sleeeeep."

All tension drained from her body. Her shoulders slumped. Her head fell to the side, her lips hung loosely and her knees fell apart.

A thrill ran through Doc's body.

"Now I want to have a good look at you." His tone was still mellow. "Slip the strap of your dress from your shoulder."

She raised her hand to the strap, slipped her thumb beneath it and moved it over her shoulder. Doc saw her breasts settle. Passion stirred deep within his body, but he constrained himself.

"Now slide the hem of your skirt up. Show me your panties."

Helen stretched her hands toward her knees. They came to rest on her smooth thighs for a moment, then her fingertips slid gently toward the hem of her skirt. She took the fabric and slowly slid it up her legs.

Doc's felt the exquisite stirring of lust. In a strange reversal, she had gained control over him, but only for the moment. Get a grip, Doc. He exhaled forcefully and refocused.

"That's it. Show me your panties."

Slowly, she inched the skirt up, until the pink panties showed between her thighs.

Doc smiled. She'll be ready in no time.

Dressed in his finest black suit, Doc passed through the wrought iron gates of White Hall. He walked along the manicured lawn toward the white, two-story Victorian mansion. He looked up at the six columns that support the porch roof and felt in his pocket for the letter. He had been summoned there by special messenger. The colonel wanted to see him.

Doc marveled at the size of the place; the porch alone was large enough to host a dance. He rubbed his sweaty palms together and approached the door. When he came near, it swung open from within to reveal a handsome, black butler. "Mr. Laurent." The butler motioned for him to enter. "The colonel has been expecting you."

"Thank you." Doc entered the foyer and stood on the oak floor.

"Wait here. I'll inform the colonel of your arrival."

Doc looked about the foyer until a large painting in a gilt frame caught his attention. He focused on the image; it was a portrait of a captivatingly-beautiful woman with her hair pulled back into a tidy bun. She wore a lacey Victorian dress and held to her breast a single red rose. She smiled the smallest, most captivating smile. Doc stood awe-struck. He had never seen an image like it. What he found most remarkable, even more moving than the entrancing smile, was the relationship between the figure and its setting. She was surrounded by a fine grey mist and appeared to materialize from it.

Doc stared at the painting, watched her slowly come into being.

"Mr. Laurent."

Doc gasped and blinked.

"The colonel will see you now."

Doc took a deep breath and let it flow out across his teeth.

"Follow me."

The butler led Doc through a large doorway into a formal living room appointed with the finest Victorian furniture and a marble fireplace. They passed through this room and another one like it, until they came to an oak door with a white, porcelain knob. The butler glanced at Doc, knocked, and entered. "Mr. Laurent to see you, sir."

"Show him in."

The butler motioned for Doc to enter. He exhaled deeply and stepped through the door to see the colonel, smiling. A wave of relief flowed through his body.

"Doc." The colonel drawled out the name as though it had two syllables. "Come in, my boy."

Doc took a second to study the colonel. He was a tall, lean, white-haired figure of proud bearing, wearing a blue and white seersucker suit with a thin bowtie. He was pure southern gentleman down to his black wingtip shoes.

Doc looked around the room and figured it would be called either a parlor or study. Along one wall, a bookshelf held countless leather-bound volumes. Bright sunlight flowed through a tall window and lit the room well enough for one to read while sitting in one of two leather wingback chairs.

"Have a seat, Doc." The colonel sat and extended a hand, smoothly indicating the other chair.

"Yes, sir." Doc moved quickly across the Persian rug to the chair.

"Bourbon?" The colonel gestured toward the small, round table between the two men.

"No, thanks."

The colonel removed the lid from a sterling ice container, took silver tongs from the tabletop and pulled out a few ice cubes. He dropped the ice into highball glasses and smiled when he heard the ice cubes clink. Then, he picked up the crystal bottle of bourbon, removed the stopper and raised it to his nose. He took a long breath to smell the aroma. "Yes." Ice shifted in the glass when the bourbon hit it. "Indeed." The colonel slid the drink across the table to Doc. "There is, my boy, an art to pouring bourbon." He smiled. "Just as there is an art to drinking it." He locked Doc with his eyes for a moment. "It's a wicked spirit, full of vile intentions." The Colonel sipped from his glass. "One must mind his Ps and Qs with this one." He smiled. "Now. Let's have a drink. Two gentlemen celebrating a great success."

Doc smiled and looked into his glass.

"To Doc, whose work has blessed me with the fairest creature thus far to walk these halls."

He gestured slightly toward Doc with his upraised glass, and the two men slowly sipped their bourbons.

"Yes, my boy, you have done a remarkable job." He stroked his white goatee and called out, "James." The butler opened the door and stepped into the room. "James, I want you to show in the lovely lady."

"Yes, sir." The butler ducked out and closed the door.

"Now, tell me how you learned your art?"

"In La Grange. I learned the methods from a book in the prison library. When I got out, I practiced on the ladies, you know, to get what I wanted but stay outta the pokey. Soon I had more girls than you could shake a stick at. All of 'em thought I looked like Brad Pitt and tasted like fine chocolate. Hell, they were fightin' over me like I was silk panties on sale."

A knock at the door. The door swung open.

"The lovely lady, sir."

"Show her in."

Doc's eyes grew large, and he took a deep breath when he saw her. She was the finest, most beautiful belle he had ever seen. He studied her from the tip of her wide-brimmed sun hat down along her slender neck, full breasts, thin waist and billowing hoop skirt.

"Extraordinary." The Colonel grinned. "You, my dear, are a work of art and a joy to behold."

"Well, thank you, sir." Her voice was lilting and sweet.

"Tomorrow you will be wed, and I shall have the pleasure of giving you away." The Colonel smiled broadly.

"Yes, sir." The belle curtsied.

"Now, see the seamstress. She will fit you for your dress."

"Yes, sir." She turned to the door, opened it and glided through.

The colonel turned to Doc. "She will make an excellent wife for my friend and fellow traveler of the left hand path, Lester Jones."

"An-dy." Meridiana whispers to him as he sleeps. "An-dy." She stands perfectly poised among toppled columns and crumbling marble statues with missing noses. Her glistening hair, smooth legs, and burgeoning hips and breasts captivate him as he walks toward her. "An-dy." She draws out his name as though she were stretching song lyrics to fill a bar of music. "An-dy." Her voice floats like vapor, billowing through the cool air of his dream to entice and intoxicate him.

Stepping up to the marble figure, he reaches out a hand to caress her ankle. A chill runs through his body when he touches her cold foot, but soon it draws warmth from him, and he strokes his cheek across her foot like a cat. Andy inhales deeply through his nose, turns his head and opens his mouth to take in one of her toes. He sucks it like a child suckling mother's nipple and runs a hand up the back of her calf, where he feels her heart beat. He sucks deeply, swallows her filth and funk, and chromosomal longing stirs his body. Nodding on her toe, he slides a hand up the back of her leg to her round bottom and kneads the thick flesh until he reaches the center and source of the world. A rush of hormones floods his body, and he loses all inhibition. He looks up at her but can't make out her face. It is just a blur. He stares and squints but quickly gives up the effort as her timeless scent envelopes him in lust.

"Andy." Carol rouses him from the dream. "You wanna get up? Take a walk?"

Andy opens his eyes to find himself in the corner chair. Carol, wearing a white tee shirt and blue panties, approaches to offer a bowl of oatmeal with a spoon sticking out of it.

Hiding his excitement, Andy takes the bowl without looking at her. "I need to work."

"Okay." Carol pulls the tee shirt over her head to reveal teardrop breasts, thin waist and small belly. "Guess I'll go to the store." She leans over to pick up a bra, puts it on, and steps into her jeans, shifting left and right to settle her bottom into them. "We need a few things."

"Sounds good." Andy stares at the painting.

"I made you some tea." Carol walks to him and kneels to look at the painting. Her muscles tense, as seething anger and jealousy makes a mockery of her tender heart. She wants to throw the hot tea on the canvas to scald the woman's petroleum flesh. She wants to shred the canvas with her nails so that even the slight inkling of being represented there exists no more. Her heart thumps against her sternum, and the cup rattles on its saucer.

Andy notices the cup shaking and looks Carol in the eyes. She gives him a pleading look, and he sees her suffering. He wants to reach out to her. He wants to comfort her, but he can't. He is committed to the other woman, his dream woman, Meridiana. "Thanks for the tea."

Carol stifles a sob and walks to the bed, sits on the edge of it, and bends over to slip on her shoes. A tear drops from the tip of her nose, falls through the air, and splashes on her brown suede shoe. She glances at Andy, entranced by the whore, and longs to be with him as they once were; happy, smiling and content. That was before she had arrived to take up residence in his dreams and dominate his art.

Carol watches Andy sketch poses and compositions. She wishes she had some talent and passion other than loving him, but she doesn't. She watches him close his eyes to envision her then open them to make a quick sketch or write some notes about her. Carol's heart aches and she quietly weeps until she falls asleep around midnight.

Andy settles into the velvet-covered corner chair and studies the painting through the night. He refines the figure, her pose and gesture. About three in the morning, Andy pours paint thinner into an empty Folgers coffee container and mixes in some white paint to make a wash. Using a large round brush, he spreads it across the entire canvas to obscure the image and provide a fresh background for a new study.

The noxious fumes of the paint thinner wake Carol, and she gets out of bed to check Andy's progress. When she sees the painting destroyed, Carol cannot hide her shock. "What are you doing?"

"This is not her. Too beautiful. Too fake. Not the real deal."

"What is the real deal?" She shakes her head. "Tell me, Andy."

"Desire unleashed." He runs a hand through his hair. "Not this pretty pin up bullshit."

"And what about me? Am I the real deal?"

"Damn it, Carol." Andy turns from her. "This is not about you."

"Isn't it?" A tear rolls down her cheek. "You spend all your time suffering over this—this woman, making this leg just so and that breast just perky enough to get you off." Carol weeps. "What about me?"

"You don't understand."

"I understand you would rather spend your time with her than me."

Andy stands for a moment, puts on his navy blue pea coat and black leather porkpie hat. He slides a hand into its pocket to find the key. "I'll be back." He walks to the door, raises the latch and slides it open. Looking back, he sees Carol, weeping on the bed. I must see Doc Laurent. He steps into a mix of sleet and rain, slides the door closed, and walks toward the Lowell on the corner.

The pitter pat of sleet against his hat and coat resembles the sound of popcorn popping, and he thinks of his mother, heating the old-fashioned aluminum pan of kernels on the stove. He recalls the top expanding, doming up, as the kernels exploded. Jiffy Pop. That's the name. I feel like I'm in a package of Jiffy Pop, and I'm a kernel of corn about to burst.

He sloshes on through the slushy slop. At the Lowell, he rounds the corner to the left, walks through the bright light, past the many images of her, waiting and tempting. For a moment, he gazes through the glass to see her manifested, objectified, and monetized. I am selling my dreams. His mind baulks at the thought. How bizarre. He looks down the street and sees the glowing southern gentleman sign and sets off toward it. I must see Doc Laurent.

Fear rises in his body as he approaches the doorman. A shiver runs along his spine, and his head vibrates as his neck stiffens. Andy feels the jagged edges of the key in his hand and hopes that he has the right place. He walks up to the doorkeeper, stands in front of him, and looks him in the eye.

"Well?"

"Doc" Andy swallows hard. "Doc Laurent." Andy glances at the door and sees the sign: Kentucky Gentlemen's Club. "Is he here?" He reaches into his pocket and retrieves the key.

"Lester Jones gave me this." He holds the key up to show the doorman, whose face softens.

"There's the door. You must open it yourself."

Andy's heart pounds and he draws a quivering breath. He steps past the dog-faced man and up to the blackened glass door. He looks at the key slot, extends the key in his shivering hand and slips it into the lock. He twists it until he encounters resistance. He applies more pressure, still it will not turn further. He lets go of it and rubs his thumb across his fingers to notice the sweat on the palm of his hand. He grips the key, applies pressure, and the lock gives.

Andy exhales deeply and feels his body slump. He turns the key back, removes it and puts it in his pocket. He rubs his sweaty palms on his jeans and reaches out his right hand to take hold of the door handle. He pulls back on the door, and it swings open to reveal utter darkness. Andy peers inside but can't see a thing. He stands for a moment, then looks back at the guard, who says without looking, "In or out."

Andy feels the cold tingle, the icy fingers of fear, tickling his spine. He swallows hard and blinks, takes a deep breath, and steps through the door, which closes behind him. Inside there is only darkness. He stands in the pitch black space and wonders what he has gotten himself into. Images of Carol flow through his mind. What have I done? He turns back, presses against the door, but finds it locked. Digging in his pocket, he searches for the key. When he finds it, he grasps it between his thumb and finger. Removing it from his pocket, Andy feels it hang and slip from his grip. A long moment later, he hears it sing out high and metallic as it bounces on the hard floor. The sound fills the hollow space, and Andy's heart sinks. A tear comes to his eye. There is no going back. Only forward. His pulse quickens, he takes a deep breath and steps into the void.

The sounds of his breath and footsteps fill the vacant space, as he moves forward until he encounters a wall. He feels it to determine that it is a corner, which turns right. Keeping his left hand on the wall, he walks until it ends, and he rounds a corner to see flickering candlelight. He walks toward it to see a glass block bar. A bartender leans on it and gestures for him to approach. "We've been expecting you."

Andy looks about to see darkness all around. Only the bar is illuminated. "What is this place?"

"It's where we gather."

"Who?"

"The Ordo."

"The what?"

"Lester can explain." He pushes up from the bar. "What'll it be?"

"Bourbon."

Andy clinks his empty glass against his others, and the bartender looks his way. "Another?" He sets a fresh glass of ice in front of him and pours in the bourbon.

From the darkness behind Andy, a figure approaches and laughs.

Andy turns to the man, emerging from the shadows into the flickering candlelight. He makes out his dark, slicked-back hair but doesn't recognize him.

"Do I know you?" Andy's heart races.

"We have business."

"What would that be?" He draws a breath between his teeth.

"I introduced you to her." He smiles. "The one you paint."

Andy looks at the man as beads of sweat form on his forehead. "Mister, you're full of shit."

"I'm Doc Laurent."

Andy studies the man's face.

"You're Doc Laurent?" His face tenses slightly.

"Just relax. You're among friends."

"Friends?"

"Yes. We all want the same thing."

"I wanted to see you but have no idea why. Isn't that strange?"

"It will be explained. All you need to do is listen." As he says this, Doc Laurent picks up Andy's empty glass and taps it with a spoon. The glass sings out, and Andy's eyelids flutter.

Andy opens his eyes to see Lester Jones standing before him. "Nice of you to join us." Lester smiles. "I suppose you are asking yourself, 'what is going on?'" He rubs his jaw with the palm of his hand, takes a candle from the bar and gestures for Andy to follow. "Come with me. I will explain everything." Lester turns away.

Andy steps from the bar stool and follows Lester into the darkness. After a brief walk, they arrive at a large, ancient-looking door, constructed of wooden planks held in place with wrought-iron hardware. Lester reaches out to the latch, lifts it and swings the heavy door, squeaking on its hinges. Andy looks through the doorway and sees, by the flickering light of Lester's candle, smooth, stone steps, leading down. Andy watches him descend a couple steps, and mounting anxiety prompts him to follow.

"You see, Andy." Lester looks back. "The woman you paint has a name. It's an ancient name from the beginning of time." Lester falls silent as he walks around the corner of a switchback landing. Andy watches the candle disappear around the corner. A chill runs through his body, and he notices the air is much colder here than on the surface. He rubs his hands together, as he rounds the corner to the left and sees light from Lester's candle.

"Pope Sylvester the second knew her name." Lester continues his descent. "He knew it well. On his deathbed, he gave her credit for his ascendance to the throne." Lester descends a few steps in silence, and the sound of scuffing shoes and dripping water fills the stairwell. "Countless others have known her, tasted her pleasures, but few have known her by name. What is her name, Andy?"

The direct question surprises Andy. *I have known her pleasures. That's true. But her name? She has a name?*

"I thought not." Lester comes to another landing and again his light disappears around the corner. "Her name, Andy, is Meridiana. She is a demon, one of Lilith's brood. She is capable of satisfying a man's every desire. Do you want power? Do you want sexual pleasure? Do you want everlasting fame? Yes. That is every artist's desire: eternal life." Lester stops. "All you have to do is submit to her, give her what she wants."

"And what is that?" Andy licks his cold lips. "She wants a child." Lester rounds another corner. "You're not the first artist to attract demonic attention." He clears his throat. "Leonardo Da Vinci was favored by Belfagore, who inspired his inventions, including the Flower of Life."

"What is that?"

"It is a geometrical design of intersecting circles. It has supernatural powers. Leonardo had two domes constructed using the design. The first was used by Cesare Borgia to capture the demon Buer, which fell into the hands of the colonel long ago. He has used it to gain power and long life. When the Osiris tower was constructed, he had the Masons install the demon in this basement."

Andy's mind reels. *He's taking me to see a demon in a cage built by Leonardo Di Vinci? This man is crazy.*

Lester reaches the end of the stairs and stands in a couple inches of standing water. Andy looks about to see that they are in an arched corridor, constructed of red bricks.

"We have the other Flower of Life dome."

"We?"

"Yes. The Ordo of Flammeus Serpens."

"Devil worshipers?"

"Call us what you will." Lester turns, and the two begin to slosh through the tunnel. The splashing sounds reverberate in the small space to create an ominous soundscape. Andy wants to know more but can barely hear himself think. They come to the end of the tunnel and enter a large, vaulted chamber, constructed of rough-hewn grey stone.

"You have the ability to conjure Meridiana."

Andy puzzles over Lester's statement. I'm no conjurer. I'm an-- The thought stops short, as Andy realizes what Lester means. "The painting. That's why you want the painting."

"Yes. You can bring her from the void." Lester smiles. "But only if you truly want." He looks Andy gently in the eyes. "I have used Doc to guide you to her, but he can't make you bring her from the darkness. Only you can do that, and you must choose to do it."

Andy stands for a moment to settle mind.

"Show me the demon."

"Follow me." Lester and Andy splash through the standing water until they walk a slight incline to a dry floor. They arrive at a dome-shaped structure covered by a canvas tarp. Lester takes the tarp in his hand and looks back at Andy, whose body tingles with anticipation. Lester throws off the tarp. It ruffles and rumbles through the air. The breeze from the moving tarp extinguishes the candle, and they stand in darkness. An acrid odor like rotten eggs mixed with burning hair assaults Andy. His stomach churns. He chokes back vomit with a hard swallow and squeezes his eyes shut to sooth the sting. Andy hears himself breathe heavily through his mouth. Pressure builds behind his eyes, and his head quivers on his tense neck. He clenches his teeth and stares into the darkness, while Lester searches his pockets for his lighter. He pulls it out and flicks the striker. A bright spark jumps from his hand to reveal briefly two red eyes. Andy jerks back, and a scraggly howl cuts through the darkness and stench. Lester strikes the flint again. This time the lighter produces a flame, which Lester extends toward the cage. Flickering light shines through the arcing bronze bars to reveal the flesh and bone form of a nightmare. Angular limbs twitch. Rotting flesh hangs. Sharp teeth snap. Andy marvels at the creature's stalking fierceness, stands in awe of its menacing power. A surge of energy runs through his body to tighten his muscles and quicken his pulse. He feels the beast's intensity in his own body. Every inch of it screams with renewed vitality and lust as though a strange new sun had just risen on a barren landscape to bring forth life. Andy drops to his knees. "I'll do it."

11

As the sun rises, Andy, drunk on bourbon and revelation, stumbles down the alley toward his studio. He reaches the grey door and leans heavily against it. His head starts to roll back, but he checks the motion, takes a deep breath and tries to compose himself, but the remembrance of the demon's snapping teeth and foul stench fill his mind like water filling a glass to the rim. Sweat beads up on his forehead, and saliva fills his mouth. He swallows hard, wraps his arms around himself and slides down the door to sit on the pavement. The door rattles loud enough to startle Carol, who waits for him inside, and she runs to the door. "Andy?"

He opens his mouth to respond but produces only a hoarse, scraping tone. Carol opens the door just a few inches, and Andy's hand falls through the gap. Seeing the hand fall by her feet, Carol jumps back, looks at it, and immediately recognizes it. Energy jolts through her body, and she heaves the door to find him shivering on the pavement. She drops to her knees and presses her cheek to his. Bone cold. "My God." Carol's heart flutters, and she cradles his head in her hands. She takes a quivering breath, and tears flow from the tip of her nose to splash on Andy's cheek.

Andy sucks a breath between chattering teeth and looks pleadingly into her eyes. Carol helps him to his feet and leads him to the bed, where he collapses. She covers him with several thick blankets and gets beneath them to share her body heat.

Andy wakes to the smell of oatmeal, rich with butter. He uncovers himself and sits up. "My head." Andy rubs his stiff neck and looks across the studio at the canvas in the corner. Am I really gonna do it? Bring her from the other side? Give her over to Lester Jones? And what does he want with her? Is he gonna run a peep show so rich assholes can beat off? Harness her power? For what purpose?

"Where were you last night?" She tries to smile but her lips quiver instead.

He rubs his face. "I went to the club."

"To meet Lester?"

Andy nods.

"So, you're gonna do the painting?"

Andy raises his eyebrows and takes a deep breath. "Yeah."

"Good. Maybe then you'll be done with her.' She looks into his eyes to perceive his reluctance. "What's wrong?"

"Nothing." Andy looks away and swallows hard. "I'm scared."

She takes him into her arms and strokes his hair.

Andy breathes deeply and relaxes slightly into her embrace.

12

"Hi, Carol." Daniel smiles. "Andy here?"

"Yes, but he doesn't feel well."

"We'll just be a minute."

"Okay." Carol glances into Helen's blue eyes and inwardly cringes. "Excuse me." She slouches toward the bathroom.

Daniel and Helen walk toward Andy, sitting in the corner.

"How's it coming along?" Daniel raises his eyebrows.

Annoyed by the interruption, Andy looks away from the canvas abruptly and glares at Daniel, but when he notices Helen his expression softens and he smiles.

"Hello, Andy." She leans her head a bit to the right and looks into his eyes. "Mind if I have a look?" Helen steps toward him. He smiles, and she walks behind him, rests her hands on his shoulders and looks at the painting. "Coming along."

"You know, Andy, it is imperative that you finish--"

"Hush, Daniel." Helen glides her fingertips up the sides of Andy's neck and leans against him. She strokes his cheeks gently, and he closes his eyes to savor the sensations. She slides her hands down his neck to his chest and across his nipples, as she presses her breasts against the back of his head. Andy reaches back to rub her leg and feels a rush of excitement.

Carol, peering through a crack in the bathroom door, watches Helen lean down to whisper into Andy's ear. Tears rush to her eyes. Helen hears her sobs, as she says, "Hyatt. Room 817."

Andy looks drunkenly into the hollow space of the Hyatt and thinks of Helen. He recalls her rubbing his chest and whispering in his ear and the rush of excitement he felt when he touched her leg. It was more than the satisfaction of desire. The thrill was unprecedented. Not even his first encounter with Carol could compare to the rising, spiraling desire he had felt. He imagines her plump red lips and sees his reflection on the convex surfaces of her shining teeth. In her presence, he had felt both helpless and profoundly empowered, constrained and liberated by desire. Her influence was extraordinary, and he feels it even now. Desire for her has led him here to the shiny interior of this echo chamber, where sound reverberates round and round, and guests come and go, but she remains steady in his mind. There will always be the other woman. The plaything or seductress will forever lead men astray. The elevator dings, and he smiles as he enters, presses eight, and looks through the glass to watch the ground floor recede.

Standing at the rail, he looks down into the open space and thinks how much it resembles the place where he encounters Meridiana. The yawning, gaping nothingness of imagination has fed, nourished, and sated him the last several years. I have been a photographer at the side of a deep lake. On the shore. Snapping images of the strange creatures. I have been a diver, swimming with her. Now I shall play the fisherman. Pull her from the depths. A strange fish, colorful and bizarre. But what has Helen to do with Meridiana? Is one a reflection of the other? Are they two sides of the same coin, or are they points on a continuum running from Carol to Meridiana with Helen located somewhere between?

The door is like all the others, smooth, wood, opaque. Only the brass numbers 817 indicate that something special waits for him on the other side, but he doesn't knock. He waits for something. Perhaps it is courage. Perhaps it is delusion. Regardless, he stands for a long moment with his knuckles poised to knock. He pulls back his hand, licks his lips and thinks of her. Flowing hair. Shining eyes. Moist lips. Supple breasts. Round hips. Memories and fantasies. Carol and Helen. He can't tell one from the other. He tries to choose. He tries to put Carol out of his mind, but she clings to him. Like a hero holding the hand of someone who has fallen through thin ice on a frozen lake, Carol clings to him. He draws an unsteady breath and recalls the vigor he felt in the presence of the demon. Energy is eternal delight. He recalls his determination to follow his chosen course to the end. He is on the left hand path. He is whiskey bent and hell bound.

Two quick knocks and a tear.

The door glides open and he sees her there. Helen, wearing only a red silk gown. He sees her supple curves and shimmering surfaces and swallows hard. Glancing into her eyes, he sees the sparkle and promise of delight. A wave of desires swells in him, and all thoughts of Carol fall away like dry leaves in a fall breeze. She smiles slightly, and he steps through the door.

She turns and walks away from him. He watches her bottom shift beneath the red silk, takes a deep breath, and licks his lips.

She sits in a wingback chair at the side of the bed and indicates another for him. Seeing only her, he follows. At this moment, he would follow her anywhere. He would follow her into a burning building, into a raging sea, into the depths of Hell. He sits, and she hands him a drink, bourbon straight. He tips the glass and looks into it to see the amber liquor, shimmering. He inhales deeply to take in its aroma. Rich and pungent, sweet and musty. He lifts the glass and tips it back, feels the liquor smooth on his tongue and harsh on his throat. She smiles.

"Do you want me?" She whispers and reaches out to touch his hand.

He looks at her, perceives a demand in her question and firm expression. He nods.

"You want the pleasure of my flesh?" She licks her lips. "You want to feel the succulence of my moist embrace?" She smiles and slides the hem of her gown up her thighs and parts her legs to expose herself. "Want to spill your seed in me?" She drags her manicured red nails through her twisty hairs and draws a sharp breath, hissing through her teeth. "There is something you must do for me first."

He swallows hard and looks at her. "Anything."

"Get on your knees." She presses her hand against herself and squeezes her thighs tight against it. She savors the sensation for a moment. "Crawl to me." She looks him in the eyes, displaying her fierce presence. "Like a dog."

Something in him recoils. Perhaps it is his pride, rising up to resist, but lust is a powerful drive. Instinctual. Primal. Indecent. It drives men to all manner of perversions and degradations, and Andy would not be the first man to approach a woman on his knees. He looks at her, leaning back, enjoying her own sensuality, and he wants the pleasure of her body. He bites his lip, draws a long breath, and pushes up from the chair.

"That's it. Be my dog."

He lowers himself onto his hands and knees, and strains his neck to look toward her. He sees her red nails showing the destination.

"Here, boy."

He awkwardly approaches and catches her scent. Drawing near, he feels the heat from her thighs on his cheeks. She reaches out to take his head in her hands and presses her thighs tight against his head.

"That's it." She lays back. "Swallow my filth."

Overcome by desire, a slave to his lust and its object, Andy feels his life force drain into her and realizes that her perverse desire is but a fraction, a pale imitation, of the dark force he intends to unleash upon the world.

"Now." She pushes his head back. "I want you in me."

He struggles to his feet, but drunkenness overcomes him, and he loses his balance. He reaches out but finds nothing to hold and falls into the nightstand. His head jerks back, as his face impacts the edge of it, and he collapses to lay in a growing pool of blood.

I can't compete with her. She has everything: beauty, wealth and Andy's attention. Carol sighs and her chest heaves. Tears flow from her eyes. Her sobs echo through the open space of Andy's studio, and she feels overwhelmed by so many images of the other woman. She looks at a painting and takes a big drink from her glass of vodka. There she lays, sprawled out, faceless and ready. Carol throws her glass at the painting. The canvas gives upon impact, and vodka splashes the image. Through tear-filled eyes, Carol watches the clear liquid flow down the canvas until unconsciousness overtakes her.

Carol wakes to the sound of a car pulling up the alley. She struggles to her feet and goes quickly to the door. She slides it open a little and squints against the sunlight to see Helen helping Andy from the passenger side of her black Mercedes. Carol notices his blood-stained shirt, and her heart sinks. She throws open the door. "Andy!" She runs to him, slides her left arm around him for support, and turns to face Helen. She looks upon her flawless beauty, and her body fills with rage. Her hands tremble, her face blushes, and her eyes fill with tears. "We have suffered enough because of you." She draws a quivering breath through her teeth. "Now, get outta my sight, you scabby whore, you home wrecker." Carol stares into Helen's eyes. She looks deeply into them to see her haughty disregard and feels her arm move with a forceful motion. Carol feels the impact of her palm on Helen's cheek and sees her head turn. "Outta my way, slut."

Mindlessly probing with his tongue the now-toothless gums at the front of his mouth, Andy looks at the canvas. He studies its textured surface, notices the brush strokes, and barely discerns the image, now obscured by the wash. It was so near perfection. What now?

He squeezes black paint from a large tube onto a pallet, dabs a large brush into it and stands for a moment. He raises the brush and smoothly draws a large circle. He stares deeply into the sacred space until his body becomes still. His mind sinks into silence, and the studio disappears from his awareness. He enters the void. Darkness, vast and complete, washes over him, engulfs him, seeps into him. Time does not exist for him here. In the world, his body rocks slowly with a certain rhythm, but here he is only awareness, and that awareness experiences one thing. Lust.

The sound of dripping water and the smell of burning hair rise up from the void to fill his vacant awareness, and he hears the sloppy sounds of something mucking through mud. Low and spidery, Meridiana skulks toward him. Her long limbs, hinged on bulbous joints, carry her smoothly toward him. She giggles and raises up to show her breasts; full and, like the rest of her, covered by smooth, red flesh. Chirping and growling, she squats before him to reveal herself. As she fondles her breasts and snaps her sharp teeth, her crotch drips juice like a beast drooling over a fresh kill. Her musty scent fills him with longing. He resists, but her force of attraction is strong, and his awareness drifts like vapor toward her. Her chirping grows louder, and he struggles desperately to form a thought. Nothing. Not a song lyric. Not a prayer. He drifts toward her, circles around her like a mist. She parts her lips to reveal sharp teeth and slowly inhales. He begins to drift into her, enters her to feel her fierce energy, jittery and electric. On the verge of total submission, Andy floats into her boundlessness, dissolves into her ecstasy. A blast of trumpets cuts through the vast emptiness, and Andy's awareness withdraws from the beast. His eyelids snap open and he gasps.

He picks up a tube of paint, squeezes a big blob of red onto his pallet and attacks the canvas with thick strokes and smears of unmixed color. Andy works frantically for about an hour. When he finishes, he steps back to study the image. A voluptuous female exposes her dripping vagina tauntingly and bares jagged teeth in a snarling display. Andy drops his brush, and a sharp pain pulses at the base of his skull.

"Get rid of it." Carol stares with disgust at the painting. "Get that thing out of here."

Andy bites his lower lip and knits his brows.

"I'm serious, Andy." She looks at him sternly. "That thing. It's hideous. It's an abomination."

Andy parts his lips and draws a quick breath as he prepares to speak.

"No." Carol cuts him off. "Please, Andy." Her voice shakes as tears come to her eyes.

Andy looks at her and feels her determination. He glances at the painting, perceives the object of his dark desire and her promise of immortality. His heart is torn between time and eternity. He studies Carol, notices her furrowed brows and quivering chin. He nods.

15

"So, you'll come to the ceremony?" Lester smiles.

"Yeah, but I need to know." Andy glances at him and looks away. "Why do you want her?"

"I'm going to conquer her. Do as I please."

"Yeah."

"I'll send a truck 'round tonight to pick it up." Lester takes a silver pen from his pocket and scribbles on a scrap of paper. "Here's the address. It's a warehouse near here. Be there at two a.m."

"One more thing." Andy rubs his cheek. "The money."

"Tonight."

Andy hears chanting, dark and monotonous, when he passes through the door into the dark space. He sees a stack of black cloaks on a table and hesitates for a moment, thinking of Carol, smiling and happy, as she once was. His heart hardens, and he resolves to follow his course to its end. He takes a cloak from the table, slides it over his head and turns his attention to the chanting. He follows the sound down a long corridor until he comes to a large, candle-lit space, where he sees several cloaked figures gathered around the Flower of Life. Andy enters the space and sees the painting inside the cage. A man wearing a red cloak stands by it. He calls out in Latin and the others chant a response. Smoke rises from the painting, and the man calls out again. The others chant their response, as Carol slips in a back door. More smoke rises from the canvas. Andy's heart pounds, and the chants grow louder. He stares at the canvas, smells the smoke to detect her succulent scent. It is her. She will soon arrive. A thrill runs through his body, and his breath quickens. Years of effort are coming to fruition before his eyes as the canvas smokes, and the group chants, and a claw tears slowly through the canvas.

The room fills with awed gasps, and the red-robed man calls out with vigor, "Nāta! Nāta! Nāta!"

Another claw grasps the slit, and the beast rends the canvas and steps majestically through it. All stand in silent awe, as the beast draws herself up to her full, seven foot height, snaps her head from side to side, and opens her gaping maw to produce a scratchy, plaintive wail. It is a sound akin to an eagle's call but longer and louder and more intense to behold. It sends shivers up Andy's spine and he falls to his knees. Several of the group turn for the exit. Their movements create a general commotion, which intensifies when she screams again. Triumphant pride turns to fear, and nervousness sweeps through the room like wildfire. The beast reaches up to touch the bars at the top of the cage. She wraps her claws around them and screams again. The horrible wail echoes through the open space, and she jerks against the circular bars. Two of them separate. She takes the loose pieces in her claws and, with great force, tears them apart.

The cloaked figures scream and rush toward the corridor, and the demon rips through the cage to emerge from the top of it. She stands upon the Flower of Life and leans her head back to scream. Leaping down from the cage, Meridiana slashes deep gashes in Daniel's face. He clutches his hands to his cheeks. Blood spews between his fingers as he rolls in agony on the concrete floor.

She turns to Lester, who shivers in place with Helen by his side.

"No." He pants. "Lord, no."

She leaps about twenty feet to land on him. He falls screaming to the floor, and she takes his head between her claws, steps on his shoulders, and leans back. His neck stretches, muscles tear and tendons pop. She growls and her eyes grow large as she wrenches his head from his body. Meridiana holds it in the air and screams. She squats over Lester's body, puts his head between her legs, and throws her head back as she slowly pushes it into herself.

Andy's body stiffens, breath hangs in his throat, and a high-pitched tone rings in his ears. He grinds his teeth, and his toes curl inside his shoes. He draws a sharp breath through clenched teeth and feels his heart pound pain into his brain.

Meridiana slowly approaches. "An-dy."

Fear grips him, and he falls to his side.

"An-dy." Meridiana steps over his prone body to straddle him, closes her eyes, and rolls her stomach like a belly dancer. The motion produces muffled crunching and popping sounds, as the beast crushes Lester's skull within her. She slides long, curving nails through her curly hairs to show herself to Andy. Blood and flesh splash onto Andy's face. He turns his head to the side and squeezes his eyes shut, as chunks of Lester's skull fall onto his cheek. Air hisses through the gap in Andy's teeth to produce blood bubbles on his lips. He cringes and whimpers on the floor beneath the demon.

Carol steps from the darkness to face Meridiana. She looks into the hideous beast's black eyes and senses her cold emptiness, her total lack of emotion, and Meridiana hisses through her jagged teeth. She drops down onto Andy, leans down to lick his face, and squats to grind her sloppy crotch on him.

"I love him." Tears flow down Carol's face.

As the beast grinds on him, Andy looks up to see Carol in her glory. He recognizes, for the first time, Carol's unwavering commitment. Regret overwhelms him, and tears stream down his bloody cheeks, as he thinks of all he has put her through with his mad quest for sensual delight and immortality.

"I'm sorry." Andy reaches a quivering hand up to Carol.

Meridiana growls and smacks Andy's cheek to gouge the flesh.

Carol gasps and, summoning all her strength of compassion and love, steps toward Andy. She reaches out to him, and he reaches out to her. Their hands touch. And the demon cuts loose with a soul-scouring scream. The beast shakes and hisses, then bounds twice and leaps toward Helen. As Meridiana sails through the air, she transforms into pure blue energy, which enters Helen's chest. The vixen falls back and, before she hits the floor, disappears in a flash of light.

Carol kneels next to Andy, gathers him to herself, and holds him tightly. She strokes his hair, and he looks up at her to see his true reason for being.

Helen

1

Darkness reigns on the Laramie plains. Darkness, broken only by the twinkle of indifferent stars and the glimmer of a sliver moon, surrounds every blade of grass, every rocky hill, every distant mountain. Darkness, hanging like a vast cloud of turpitude, spreads over every saloon, every gambling hall, every church. Darkness, nearly complete, settles on two riders bound for town.

The silhouettes of two mounted cowboys ride side by side, bouncing like puppets across the nothingness of grassland.

Horace Gruen, a Texan of German descent, wears a Stetson as he rides on the right. He is wiry and awkward in the way only an adolescent cowboy could be. He bounces stiffly in rhythm with the patter of ropes and a bed roll.

J.C. Garcia, a Vaquero, wears a sombrero as he rides on the left near freshly-laid rails. The broad, flat brim bounces loosely as his bulky body surges with a masculine grace in response to his paint's powerful movements.

Looking down the tracks, J.C. follows their converging lines into the vast expanse of invisible prairie until his eyes reach Laramie, shimmering on the horizon like an unholy mirage. Gazing at the distant, glimmering city, J.C. feels the stirring of lust. It burns in his muscles, circulates through his veins, and tingles in every nerve. He pulls the reins to stop Stella, and Horace stops his blue roan, Orville.

J.C. pulls a pouch of Red Man tobacco from the pocket of his scuffed leather vest, stuffs a wad of chaw into his jaw, and packs it tight with his tongue. He chews it a few times, sucks at it, spits a dark stream of juice, and wipes the back of his hand across his stubbly face. "Lookie there." He gestures a little with his hand. "Look how she glows with light from all them gamblin' halls and whorehouses."

Horace peers toward the distant glimmer and sees in it the answer to his prayers and satisfaction of his desire to become a man like his father had been and J.C. is, a rough and ready man of the world. His heart aches with a mixture of fear and excitement, as he pulls a Bull Durham from the pocket of his denim jacket and puts it between his lips. Cocking his head to the left, he strikes a match on the saddle horn, lights the cigarette, and draws on it. The end glows cherry red, casting warm light across his straight nose, smooth jaw, and yellow brown eyes. Stifling a cough, Horace takes the cigarette between slender fingers, pulls it from his lips, and exhales a long cloud of smoke into the cold air. "Never seen it at night." He rubs fingertips across his forehead. "It's a whole 'nother place."

"Yeah." J.C. adjusts his sombrero. "After tonight, you'll be a whole 'nother person. Them whores gonna make a man of you." J.C. spits, and the mixture of saliva and tobacco juice splashes onto the golden grass.

Light from Laramie flickers on Horace's eyes, and he wishes he could stand to chaw so he could spit like J.C. He just doesn't have the stomach for it, so he smokes instead. Holding the cigarette between two fingers, he raises it to his lips, draws on it, and feels the smoke fill his lungs. He exhales a long cloud, and his mind drifts to the warning Mr. Goodnight had given him about going into town. He remembers his boss' words plainly. "Steer clear of that place. It's run by a band of Confederates with no respect for human life. They'll kill ya for the silver in your teeth and dump yer body outside of town."

He recalls the story the ranch owner had told him and raises the subject with J.C. "Heard them Moyer brothers have a woman hostage."

"Yeah." J.C. nods. "Girl named Annabelle." He rubs his cheek. "Mistress of some railroad boss. Holdin' her ransom, but he won't pay."

"So why mess with them?" Horace knits his brows and quickly raises the cigarette to his lips.

"They got the best whores."

With a click of his tongue, J.C. rouses Stella toward town.

Horace watches him ride away to leave him alone on the dark prairie. His hands tense on the reins, and he swallows hard. He wishes he hadn't come with J.C. So what if it's my fourteenth birthday? So what if he had promised me my first whore? Is that a life or death matter?

Apparently it is to J.C., for he intends to ride straight into the heart of darkness. He is bound for the Moyers' stronghold, the center of their corrupt reign. J.C. is leading Horace to the "Belle of The West." To J.C., the threat of death is but a kicker, a bit more thrill to sweeten the pot.

Horace's mind oscillates between a well-founded fear of the Moyers and a vague but insistent desire for the unknown delights of sex and whiskey. The joys of men call to him, entice him. What is a young man to do except follow desire to its satisfaction? Horace settles his mind, sets his sights on the retreating J.C., and spurs Orville sharply. Aboard the galloping steed, Horace focuses on his jingling spurs, notices the cold emptiness of their ringing jangle in contrast to the thud of hooves and the brush of his holster against his thigh. Riding up to J.C., Horace slows his horse to match his pace and looks over to J.C. He notices his bent nose beneath shining hazel eyes and observes the way his body bounces to absorb Stella's jolting movements. Horace lets his shoulders slouch, and his body begins to surge along with Orville's movement. How will it feel to make love to a woman? Will I be good at it? Will it make a man of me? Will I finally get J.C.'s respect?

Without speaking, the two ranch hands approach Laramie. A hundred yards outside of town, the grass of the prairie gives way to mud. Horace listens to the slopping of the horses' hooves and gradually becomes aware of the low rumble of men, groaning and shouting and laughing. Voices mingle with the clicking clatter of roulette wheels, and he finds the resulting drone out of place with the chirping of crickets.

The sound persists, growing more intricate and mesmerizing. Horace feels it reverberate through his bones and tingle through his limbs. Sinking deeper into it and the moment and the place, he notices the foul smell of death. He licks his lips to taste rotten meat, metallic on his tongue, and exhales forcefully, instinctively resisting the invasion. His lungs fill again with the tainted air. A chill travels his spine, his stomach churns, and he reins Orville to a stop. Slumping in his saddle, Horace swallows hard to fight off the urge to vomit and draws another breath through clenched teeth. His head swims with dizziness, and he struggles to maintain balance in the saddle.

J.C. spits. "Ya okay, kid?"

Horace runs a palm across his cheek and blows a breath. The stench of death, viscous and all-invasive, clings to him, smears across his cheek, and fills his lungs like the hazy film of cigarette smoke. He looks to J.C., studies his moonlit visage for a moment and imagines his father's kind eyes flashing from a shallow grave south of Denver. They peer from the beyond of his memory and imagination into his awareness in an infinite feedback loop of life and death. Horace feels for his pistol, a deathbed gift from his father. He caresses the arcing wooden handle of the Griswold and reconciles himself, for the moment, to this world tainted by death and blood.

"Yeah."

"Let's go." J.C. clicks, and Stella takes off. Horace spurs Orville.

Slopping through the muddy street past Miller's meat shop, Horace notices a streetwalker with a twisted face, ruby red lips, and bulbous breasts, spilling from the top of her black bustier. She catches his eye and calls out to him. "Hey, cowboy." She lifts her dirty skirts to reveal her chubby, scab-spotted legs. "Wanna waller 'roun' my sweet spot"

Studying the street whore, Horace feels a mixture of excitement for her ready availability and revulsion at her appearance. He presses his eyes shut, puts her out of his mind, and they continue down Front Street. Their horses' hooves leave deep craters that quickly fill with a foul mixture of water and blood and piss, glistening in the yellow light.

The two continue past unconscious drunks lying in the slop of Front Street and a snake oil salesman extoling the merits of Rousseau's Laudanum. He calls it a "gift from God," and Horace wonders what kind of god would need this huckster to shill his blessings. Once past the prophet's covered wagon, Horace sees a group of drunken soldiers from Fort Sanders.

He watches them lean on each other and sway as a group. Left then right they lean, then, like whiskey from a bottle, they pour from the street into "John Bull's" tent.

Riding between ox-drawn wagons and horses standing at random angles on the sides of the street, Horace is taken aback by the chaos of the place. There seems to be no order to the assorted tents, log cabins, and clapboard buildings, no structure except the street, running a somewhat straight line toward a huge tent. Much as a church or cathedral serves as a central point in an established, tamed, and civilized city, the tent stands out as the center of the chaos of Laramie.

The peak of the tent reaches thirty feet, and the whole triangular façade glows with the lantern light from within. The name of the saloon stands out in stark contrast. Large, hand-painted, black letters declare this to be the "Belle of The West."

They ride up to a hitching rail and dismount. Their hand-tooled boots splash in the mud, and the elaborate designs of eagles and snakes and stars disappear beneath a foul layer of gooey slop.

"Yes, sir, Horace is gonna get some tonight." J.C. whoops and leads the way down the pine boards. They walk, spurs jingling, past drunks slumped over empty whiskey barrels, to the large double door. Just as J.C. reaches toward the door flaps, a man bursts through from within. Blood flows down his face and smears the canvas flap. A deep gash stretches across his forehead, and the wound gapes open to reveal the bone beneath. The man thumps down, his face skidding on the rough pine boardwalk, and laughter erupts from the "Belle."

Horace stands still, feeling his heartbeat and looking at J.C.

"Let's go, kid." J.C. pushes through the bloody flaps into the saloon.

Horace follows.

2

Fifty or so men, standing three-deep at the rough-hewn pine bar, turn silently toward the new arrivals. Dirty ranch hands, rail men, prospectors, and townies, wearing bowlers, kepi caps, and slouch hats, study J.C. and Horace.

J.C. unconsciously rubs the leather of his holster, feels its smooth surface with his fingertips and shifts his eyes left and right to meet one stern gaze after another. He notices, behind the bar, in a corner, and at the faro table, heavily armed men wearing Confederate Army hats. He marks these men as threats.

Horace's eyes jump all about the saloon. He sees the bleary-eyed faces of drunks scowling behind bristling beards, the bulging breasts and crudely-painted faces of whores, and the metallic flash of candlelight on gunmetal. His heart races, pumping cold fear through his veins, and his shoulders slump as he sinks in upon himself and turns toward J.C.

The men in the saloon turn away, and Horace's nerves, which had been jumping and tingling, settle slightly as his heartbeat and breathing slow. He secretly longs to turn back, leave this intimidating place and return to the ranch, where Mrs. Goodnight would make him a rhubarb pie if he asked her nicely.

The saloon fills with the din of many voices, and Horace hears a mixture of accents. Irish, Scottish, and English immigrants as well as homegrown Americans from both North and South crowd around the bar to call for their drink of choice. Some call for the "special," a particularly noxious concoction of house-made rotgut cut with black powder and turpentine. The wealthier patrons order Tennessee whiskey or Kentucky bourbon, while one taste-conscious patron calls for a mixture of whiskey and blackberry liquor called a "Mule Skinner."

Horace notices the flickering candles and glowing lanterns mounted on the exposed posts of the side walls. His eyes follow the wooden frame up to the top of the tent and back at least a hundred feet to the back wall. He is nearly overwhelmed by the vastness of the enclosed space and the oppressive fear and dread that circulate within.

"There's a table." J.C. glances toward the back of the saloon.

Horace nods quickly.

The two walk past the faro and poker tables to take seats at a table made of heavy slabs of pine set atop an empty whiskey barrel.

Horace looks about the saloon, scanning for working girls. He finds them standing in a row like cattle at an auction. He looks them over, shifts his gaze left and right from one to the next. He studies this one's lips and that one's breasts and another's legs. Each has her fine points, but on the whole they are sorry scraps of women, worn out and used up shreds of femininity, nearly rubbed out by abuse and neglect.

His eyes light upon a black-haired, blue-eyed dove. Her face is less contorted than the others, and she, being new to the trade, is less jaded, less stringent and more scared than scary. He studies her and notices that her cheeks and lips, proud and full, are not painted as boldly as those of the other whores. They are a natural pink, a hue of health and sensual delight only clownishly copied by the soiled doves. Horace takes her in, breathes her life force into his lungs to displace the foul scent of death that had greeted him at the edge of town.

A woman approaches the table. "What'll it be, fellas?" She looks at Horace and smiles with her eyes.

"The woman."

"The one you were watchin'?"

"Yeah. Blue eyes." Horace looks away. "What's her name?"

"That's Justine." She smiles. "She's new. Ya like her?"

Horace blushes.

"Guess so." She bites her lip. "Kinda busy right now. Care for a drink while ya wait."

"Yeah." Horace blinks. "Bourbon."

"The good stuff?" She raises her brows.

"Yeah."

"Make it a bottle," J.C. adds, feeling a bit ignored.

The saloon girl heads back to the bar and quickly returns with a dark brown bottle of S.T. Suit Salt River Bourbon and two short glasses. She sets them on the table, and J.C., smiling to Horace, reaches out for the bottle. He looks at the label. "All the way from Jefferson County, Kentucky." J.C. smiles and pulls the cork from the round bottle. He pours two shots of the amber liquor and slides one toward Horace. "Saluda."

Horace takes the glass in his slender hand, slides it across the rough tabletop and lifts it up to notice candlelight shimmering on it and the bourbon. He puts it to his lips and tips it back slowly. The liquor flows smoothly across his tongue, and he tastes the buttery caramel flavor followed by an intense burn. He smiles, taps the end of a cigarette on the table, and strikes a match on the rough yellow wood to light the Bull Durham. He draws on it and lets smoke drift from his mouth like fog from a warm lake on a cold morning. Looking at J.C., Horace raises the glass to his nose to smell the musty scent of roses and rich earth, finishes the bourbon, and pours two more.

J.C. smiles and, laughing quietly, shakes his head.

"Saluda." Horace raises his glass and drinks quickly. A bit of the liquor escapes his mouth and flows down his smooth chin. Squeezing his eyes shut, he swallows hard, shakes his head a bit, and wipes the liquor away with his fingertips.

"J.C."

"Yeah."

"Do you remember my mother?"

J.C. studies Horace for a moment. "Yeah."

"What was she like?"

J.C. rubs his face and drinks. "She was a great cook." He raises his brows. "She made great biscuits, flaky and moist. Her chili con carne was the best. Spicy with peppers and chunks of juicy beef. All the cowpokes loved it." J.C. licks his lips. "Pork chops too. She coated 'em with flour and fried 'em in a skillet 'til they were golden brown and juicy." He presses his lips together. "But she was tender. Too tender fer frontier life." He nods slowly. "She had an artist's heart. Like a child, she lived on emotions. She needed John by her side, needed his comfort and strength, but he was a rambler, a soldier, and a cowboy. She knew it from the start." He rubs his cheek. "Kinda lost her wits when John went on cattle drives. Worried herself sick that he'd been killed or injured. And she had you to care for. A beautiful woman alone with a child on the panhandle." J.C. finishes his drink and pours two more, watches the amber liquor flow. "Anyway, she was a good woman. She just needed more attention than John could give her, and this world was far too hard for the likes of her." J.C. looks into his drink. "Do you remember what she told you on her deathbed?" He looks at Horace and rubs his stubbly jaw. "You were just a child then."

"Yeah." Horace bites his lip. "She told me to live for love. Said true love could transform the filth and pain of this world.

Make a man strong against its corruption." The dark liquor takes hold, and Horace loses the thread of his thoughts. He falls silent and sinks deeper into the dull rumble of the saloon.

After a moment of reflection, he looks about to see his chosen woman talking to another man. Jealousy rises, as he watches her walk alongside the man to a side exit. He had set his sights on her and bent his being in her direction. Now she leaves with another man. Staring at him, watching him run a hand across her round bottom, Horace finishes the drink. J.C. pours another, and Horace reaches quickly for it.

"You have your father's jealousy." J.C. bites his lip. "And his love of drink." He nods. "Be careful of that."

The saloon spins around Horace, and he feels a creeping presence from behind. He turns to see a tall man. J.C. raises his face sharply toward the fellow and sees, behind him, two Confederates with their hands on their pistols.

Horace looks up at the man and feels like a child about to get the switch. His heart thumps heavily, and he pants.

The man smiles falsely. "Boss Asa wants a word with you." The words hiss through his gaping teeth.

"Me?" Horace pulls his head back and squints. "What about?"

"Business."

J.C. stands.

"Not you." He locks J.C. with a fierce gaze, and the two Confederates draw their pistols from their leather holsters.

J.C. rubs the tips of his fingers together but swallows the urge to draw his Colt 1860. His chances are nil against two men with their guns already trained on him.

The Confederates gesture with their pistols for J.C. to sit. He looks into their cold eyes and feels the threat of their guns. His blood turns cold in his veins, and he sits. He looks at

Horace, really takes him in. Horace returns J.C.'s gaze, and his heart aches.

J.C. nods and looks away.

Horace stands and notices that he barely comes to the tall man's shoulder. The man gives him a shove toward the back of the saloon, and he walks slowly toward the red curtain. As he walks, Horace feels the overpowering presence of the man behind him, and his heart sinks deep into the pit of his stomach to gnaw and nag him with a strong and growing urge to fight. His arms tingle with fierce energy, and he feels the weight of his pistol on his side. He rubs his fingertips together and imagines pulling his Griswold to level the barrel of the revolver at the big goon. He wants to pull the trigger to splatter his guts across the pine floorboards. Certainly this would lead to his death, but anything would be better than to pass through that curtain to meet with Asa Moyer.

He catches sight of a soiled dove, sees care and concern in her eyes, and decides to risk it. Perhaps, one day, he would have her to hold and caress.

The man stops Horace at the curtain and holds out his massive hand. "Your weapon." Thick fingers curl in a beckoning gesture.

A chill travels Horace's spine, and he casts a glance to J.C.

"Give it," he commands. "Nice and slow."

3

The tall man parts the curtains with a wide sweep of his right hand. A smile stretches his scruffy cheeks, as the smell of blood and tears wafts through the opening to surround them. Horace's his muscles slowly contract and stiffen until he has to struggle to draw a quivering breath. His heart thumps, and his body tingles. The man presses his left hand firmly between Horace's shoulder blades, and Horace resists the urging force, presses back out of the primal instinct to survive.

Peering through the opening, Horace sees, in a dark corner, the bars of a jail cell. Something move beyond the bars. Something struggles in the dark. He stares at the thing and slowly realizes it is a woman on her hands and knees. She is dressed in rags of satin and lace. It had once been a fine dress in the Victorian style but now is the slightest covering of filthy shreds of fabric. Her golden hair hangs in strands to conceal her eyes. As she struggles to turn toward him, Horace sees in her upturned face an expression of deep suffering and a deeper empathy for him.

The goon shoves Horace through the opening. He regains his balance with a large step forward, but now a fellow with an eye patch and a big-headed strong man take him by the arms. The thugs force him into a chair at a large pine table. He looks across the table's rough surface to see Boss Asa Moyer, an unnaturally-thin, frail, splotchy man with fine dark hair. Asa meets Horace's gaze with cold indifference, and Horace feels his bulging eyes pry into his soul like a prospector staring into a pan of gravel in search of gold.

A woman emerge from the darkness behind Asa. As she enters the light, Horace sees her clearly, and his mind becomes entangled in the mass of black hair piled up on the top of her head and hanging down in cascades of curls. Her blue eyes appear large and her lips plump and soft. He notes the graceful curve of her neck where it meets her shoulders and the wisps of hair that hang there to brush her fair skin. He studies the round thrust of her high cheek bones and the broadness of her eyes, accented by black eyeliner. His heart longs for her as he studies the curves of her body. Her buxom bosom presses against the red satin of her bodice, and her round hips, accented by a corseted waist, swivel as she bends to whisper in Asa's ear.

He nods. "Yes, Helen."

She stands, licks her lips, and looks Horace in the eyes.

He breathes her in, consumes her image. Every cell in his body longs for and cries out to her. For a moment his mind goes blank as darkness descends on him. Slowly, it engulfs him. His heart slows, and his vision blurs as he drifts deeper into a vortex of lust. When thought returns, Horace notices on the tabletop a hunting knife. The spotted, matt-grey blade points toward him. He wants to grab it and thrust it into Asa's bloodshot eye. He wants to stab it through the fleshy sphere into his brain and watch him writhe on the end of it. He wants to stand over Asa Moyer's dead body with Helen by his side. His hands sweat with the thought, and he licks his lips as he studies the stained blade.

"Havin' a good time?" Asa reaches out his bony, spotted hand to take the knife from the table. Candlelight glints off the blade as he turns the knife around in his hand. "Allow me to make the introductions." Asa smiles. "I'm the mayor of Laramie. That man there, the cyclops to your left, he's Bloody Steve, Marshall." He chuckles a guttural, sickly, sticky laugh. "And the man to your right is Con Wager." He coughs. "Justice of the Peace. This is our saloon, and you are our guest. So, welcome. You really should try your luck at the faro table." The mayor smiles. "Might get lucky." He shrugs. "Might not. For now, you can try your luck with me." Asa studies the tip of the knife. "Gimme his gun hand."

Fear rushes through Horace like flood waters through a mountain gorge, and he tries to jump up but jolts against the henchmen's hands. The heels of his boots slide across the floorboards beneath him, and the two thugs press him down into the creaking wooden chair.

Con takes Horace's right forearm in his hand and pulls on it, but Horace resists, and Con can't lift his hand from his lap. Horace turns his face a bit to the right to look into his eyes. He sees weakness and fear and knows he could take him in a fair fight, but Bloody Steve steps behind Horace, wraps his arm around his throat, and squeezes.

Horace's face flushes, and his arm gradually weakens until Con, looking to Asa for approval, lifts his clenched fist onto the tabletop.

"That weren't so hard." Asa leans over the table and taps Horace's fist with the side of the knife. "Open it." He jabs the top of his hand, and the tip penetrates the flesh to impact bone beneath. Instinctively, Horace opens his hand and rolls it flat onto the tabletop. Asa strikes again, jabbing the tip of the knife into the top of Horace's hand to slice a large vein, standing out beneath the skin. Blood spurts from the wound and flows around the knife blade.

Horace stifles a grunt, and Bloody Steve laughs.

"You come from the Goodnight Ranch?" The boss pushes the knife a bit deeper, and Horace nods.

"Nice place." Asa smiles to reveal brown teeth. "Lots of prime pasture for those longhorns. They can graze themselves silly on all that grass by the river." Horace feels the knife tip dig deeper to gouge between bones. "Yeah, buddy, that's one fine place. Right next to my own." Asa twists the knife, and Horace feels the bones separate. "It's a shame about the fire." Asa, shaking with effort, presses hard on the handle, and the blade passes through Horace's hand. He squirms in his seat. He doesn't scream or gasp, but anguish fills his eyes.

Asa licks his chapped lips and adjusts his grip on the knife handle. He picks up a hammer from the tabletop to hit the hilt of the knife and drive the tip into the wooden table, and Horace bucks. "It's a damn shame the way that fire is gonna ravage his fields and that nice house he and his wife live in." Asa rocks the knife back and forth, and the cold steel blade scrapes against the bones and slices through tendons and ligaments. Blood flows across his hand onto the table to soak into the yellow wood. "Tell that old man to get in here with the deed." Breathing heavily and pushing his greasy hair away from his bug eyes, Asa pulls the knife from the table. "Get out."

Horace grimaces as he lifts his mangled hand from the tabletop and turns to see Con and Bloody Steve, smiling broadly. He steps between the two bullies, takes a deep breath, and parts the curtains. He looks to his right for J.C. but doesn't see him. His eyes flash toward the door, and he walks, holding his hand at his side to leave a trail of blood across the mud-smeared boards to the double-wide door. He pushes through the flaps, smearing them with blood, and looks to his right to see the horses. As he approaches Orville and Stella, he notices Stella has a load. He strains his eyes to see the glint of moonlight on jagged metal spurs.

Rushing to Stella, he finds J.C.'s body lying across the saddle.

4

Horace lifts J.C.'s head to look into his lifeless hazel eyes and his chest tingles and the blood drains from his cheeks. He closes his eyes and presses his lips together. His body quakes, and he feels all eyes upon him. Every drunken stranger, every leering whore and snake oil salesman watches him, judges him, sizes him up.

Horace hastily ties a lead to Stella and mounts Orville. He turns the horses in the slop and sets off down Front Street. Riding slowly, he looks left and right to see the faces of men hideously transformed. They have somehow lost their humanity and appear disfigured, contorted, and strange. Looking to his left, he sees a scuffle in a dark alley-like space between "John Bull's" and Hewitt's drugstore. A large man with bulging muscles holds another man by the lapels. The brutish man shakes the other fellow violently, throws him to the ground, and reaches a hand into his mouth.

Horace feels for his Griswold but doesn't find it in his holster, and a deep ache fills his heart.

He rides slowly into the stench of death at the edge of town, passes the meat market whores, and Stella follows as J.C.'s blood flows through her chestnut coat.

Out of town, onto the prairie, into the darkness, Horace rides in a solitary procession on the infinite range. He rides in the general direction of the Goodnight Ranch but feels lost, disoriented, and inconsequential beneath indifferent stars and sliver moon.

Overcome by grief and pain, Horace lays on Orville's neck, and his blood, tears, and memories flow.

J.C. had ridden with Horace and his father, John Gruen, when they had set out from Fort Belknap Texas with 2000 head of cattle. He was one of about twenty cowpunchers who pushed the herd across the Staked Plains of central Texas to Horsehead Crossing, where they had crossed the Pecos River into New Mexico and followed it north to Fort Sumner. Then, when they had pushed northward through Pueblo and were riding toward Denver with the Rocky Mountains on their left, they were ambushed by a small band of Comanche Indians.

It rained hard, and the Comanche rode, whooping and screaming, out from a draw to attack the men from behind. Several cowpokes and cows fell in the initial onslaught of arrows. The Indians shot one cowboy through the face. The arrow entered his left cheek to shatter his teeth and pass through the other side. Blood filled his mouth and the gaging cowpoke lost his balance. He fell from his horse onto the wet grass, and stampeding cattle trampled him to death.

They skewered another man with a long spear. The cowboy had been riding at the rear of the drive to round up strays, when he heard a whooshing sound and felt his body thrust forward with the impact of the large flint tip. The blade exited his chest in a bloody explosion, and the man fell from his saddle, but his right foot hung in the stirrup, and the galloping horse dragged the slain cowboy across the prairie.

Horace rode behind his father and J.C. as they turned to fight the painted warriors. John pulled two Griswolds from his holsters as he charged into the oncoming Comanche. J.C. pulled his shining Winchester 1866 rifle from his saddle-mounted scabbard. He held the yellow boy steady with one hand and followed into the fray.

Horace followed the two men, tried to keep up with their charging steeds. He felt the pounding of horse and cattle hooves, heard the sharp report of Winchesters and the loud boom of Griswolds over the caterwauling of Indians. His body jostled in the saddle as Orville charged up a hill behind John and J.C. He saw his father shoot with both hands and J.C. cut loose with the Winchester and spin it with his right hand to reload. The three charged into the ranks of savages, and Indians fell from their horses to the hard earth.

Horace saw an Indian ride straight for his father with war club raised. John was focused on shooting another attacker, but J.C. spotted the rapidly-approaching warrior. When the Indian had closed to within five feet of John, J.C. turned in his saddle and shot. The 44-caliber bullet struck the Indian in the chest, and he flew from his galloping horse. Horace saw a mist of blood spray from the Indian's bare chest and hang in the air like a small red cloud. For a moment, Horace saw only the cloud of blood and his father, riding with J.C. at his side.

Then John slowed, and Horace saw the arrow sticking through his back. His heart jumped in his chest, as he rode up to his wounded father. J.C. reigned Stella to an abrupt halt and fired from the saddle at the retreating Indians. Horace jumped from Orville and ran to his father's side. John reached out, and Horace helped him to the ground.

He looked into his father's kind face, saw the suffering in his twitching eyes. He pressed his hand around the arrow to feel blood: warm and slick.

"Take my guns." John looked Horace gently in his eyes.

Tears flowed down Horace's smooth cheeks, as he took the heavy revolvers from his father's chilled hands.

"Never." John struggled for one last breath. "Never give up." His face and hands went limp.

Beneath the grey sky, Horace kneeled over his father as a vast anguish welled up in his body. He wept. Tears mixed with rain to flow down his quivering cheeks, and his body quaked with loss and despair. He collapsed onto his father's body, laid against it in a final moment of communion, then, rising to his feet, pressed the guns against his chest.

J.C. helped Horace dig a shallow grave in the foothills of the Rocky Mountains, and they buried John Gruen beneath a simple wooden cross and the empty sky.

Horace gave one of the Griswolds to J.C., and they continued the drive to Wyoming, where J.C. and Horace stayed on with Mr. Goodnight.

In the dark of night, Orville carries Horace and leads Stella, with the body of J.C. Garcia draped across her, through the gate of the Goodnight Ranch. Reaching the main house, Horace falls from Orville. He slams to the ground and lays in a crumbled heap, as the moon moves slowly across the star-speckled sky, and his body heat drains into the cold earth.

Morning comes, and Mrs. Goodnight, a white-haired woman in her sixties, walks slowly onto the porch to find Horace, unconscious on the ground. She assumes he is drunk, until she sees the body of J.C., lying across the saddle. Mrs. Goodnight calls for her husband, who arrives promptly. Mr. Goodnight, a sturdy man at seventy, walks to J.C. and feels his cold face to determine he is dead. Kneeling, he feels Horace's cheek and discerns a slight warmth. He rolls Horace's nearly-stiff body, shakes him, and smacks his face sharply. The young man draws a shallow breath.

"He's alive!"

"I'll get a blanket." Mrs. Goodnight runs inside.

Taking Horace's head into his lap, Mr. Goodnight rubs his stiff cheeks and notices his ruined hand. He looks at the gaping wound and knows they have been to town.

Mrs. Goodnight returns with a colorful rick rack patterned wool blanket. She wraps it around Horace to warm him. At length color and plasticity return to his flesh. As his consciousness returns so does his pain, shooting up his arm fast and fierce like lightening striking a tree.

He holds his mangled hand out for the misses to see and manages to say a single word. "Asa."

5

Sitting at the poker table in the "Belle of The West," Electus "Domino" Lanham shifts his eyes to spot the confederates and his backup. Here I sit with two aces. He draws a deep breath. Both of them clubs. His heart thumps, and he struggles to keep a straight face as he glances at the three other players around the table.

"I'll raise twenty Marthas." The cheat runs up the bet, hoping to keep his hand a secret so he can take his deck and go. He runs a hand along his neatly-trimmed salt and pepper beard and stares at the man to his right.

"I'm out." He throws down his cards. Domino draws a deep breath and turns his eyes to the stone-faced man across from him. Charles Dumas is no novice gambler and he will not be scared away by a clumsy bluff. He studies Domino through squinting eyes, licks his lips, and reaches toward his stack of ones.

While Charles thumbs through his stack, fear rises in Domino. Energy courses through his body, and his hands tingle. He takes a long breath, and a bead of sweat flows down his cheek. He flashes a glance to his accomplice, James Worth, a sturdy black-haired man, standing at the bar. Shifting his gaze back toward the table, Domino sees Bloody Steve's eye staring between the curtains.

"Call." Charles throws a stack of crumpled paper bills onto the pile in the center of the table. Domino looks quickly at the money and shifts his gaze back to Bloody Steve. The two men stare, and Domino's consciousness narrows to his cold grey eye. A chill travels his spine, energy builds in his limbs, and he draws a sharp breath through his teeth.

Cutting loose with a long yell, Domino jumps from his chair. He hears it skitter across the floorboards as he flips the tabletop into the air. He sees it rise to block Bloody Steve's view. Money and cards flutter toward the floor, and he turns for the door. The smooth soles of his boots slide on the mud-smeared boards as he crosses the floor and lurches for the bloody flaps. He pushes through, crosses the boardwalk, and leaps the low rail to land next to a horse. The horse kicks him in the chest. Air rushes through his lips, and he struggles to regain his footing in the slop of Front Street.

The three other players arrive to stomp and kick the "dirty cheat."

Domino rolls over to his back, curls up his legs, and covers his head with his arms. He feels each kick as a dull thud, which knocks him about in the mud. A strong kick knocks his arms away from his face, and he sees James fly through the air to land on the backs of two of the men. The gamblers and James fall to the mud and begin scrapping, as a crowd of men flow from the "Belle" to cheer not one side or the other but action and violence in general.

The brawlers, covered with mud and blood, grab for any handhold, scratch any skin, and punch any identifiable enemy. The crowd goes wild, pumping their fists and calling for more blood. Domino hears, above the din of the crowd, a bellowing voice.

"You men." Marshall Bloody Steve exits the saloon, ducking his head so as not to hit the door frame. "You men pipe down."

The brawling and cheering continue.

The crowd parts, and Bloody Steve, hands filled with matching Colt 1860s, walks to the edge of the action. He stares into the writhing, mud-coated mass and raises the eight-inch steel barrels toward the rumble.

Boom!

The crowd goes silent and rush away, but the brawl continues.

"God damn it!" The Marshall stares fiercely through the gun smoke at the writing bodies before him. "I'm the laaaaaaw!"

The brawlers struggle to free themselves.

Marshall Long fires again. Domino sees the black powder smoke rise from the muzzle and, through it, Bloody Steve's grinning face. He hears a rapid succession of shots and the groans of those around him. One last shot rings out, and a hot bullet rips through the flesh of his left shoulder. Pain rushes through his body, and darkness overcomes him.

Searing pain wakes Domino. He struggles to breathe and pushes against a heavy weight on his chest. His hand slides across the slippery mass, and he sees by the feeble light of the sliver moon that it is the body of James Worth, shot through the head. The right side of his face is missing. Domino looks into the gaping hole that had been his friend's face and struggles frantically from beneath the body. He gets to his feet and looks about to find himself in a gully with cold bones and fresh corpses as companions. He reaches for his Philadelphia Derringer but finds it and his cash missing.

Domino presses his right hand against his shoulder, grimaces with pain, and looks up at the pale moon. He stares at it, feels its white light penetrate his soul, and he starts walking to the east. He has no destination in mind. He just wants to get away from this place of death.

6

Propped against the headboard of the small bed, Horace hears gentle knocking at the door. He looks to see it glide open and Mrs. Goodnight's head poke through. Looking at her face, surrounded by wavy white hair, Horace feels the caring gaze of her brown eyes and manages a slight smile when she speaks.

"Mornin,' child." She steps into the room. "How'd ya sleep?" Carrying a handful of white, cotton fabric, she walks slowly to his bedside and holds out her hand. "Let's have a look."

Horace grimaces and shakes his head.

"Come now." She smiles gently. "You don't have to look, but I do."

He licks his lips and lifts his right arm, which shakes from the effort.

Horace watches her slowly untie the bandage and unwind it to reveal the brown stains. He notices her furrow her brows as she pulls the material and feels it break free from the crust of dried blood and pus. A fresh rush of cold air hits the broad wound, and he draws a sharp breath through his teeth.

"Sorry." Mrs. Goodnight studies his swollen fingers, round with taut skin like sausages. The youngster watches her move a wash basin from the bedside table to the bed next to his leg. Lowering his hand into the basin, she takes a bottle of whiskey from the tabletop and removes the cork. Mrs. Goodnight pours the whiskey over his ruined hand. Horace leans his head back, bites his lower lip, and clenches his good hand into a fist. Time dilates, stretches out like a spider's web in a breeze, as each heartbeat brings a fresh onslaught. She turns his hand over to pour the liquor onto the swollen palm. Horace groans and glances up at her to see a tear hanging on the tip of her nose.

He looks into the tear and feels her loving care for him. When the tear falls, Horace feels her squeeze his mangled hand. Pus oozes from both sides of his hand to soak into the cloth and fill the room with its foul scent. Dabbing with the cloth, Mrs. Goodnight wipes away the yellow goo.

Mr. Goodnight walks into the small room to stand by his wife as she wraps a loop of fabric around Horace's hand. Horace looks at the man and notices the thin skin of his hands.

"The infection is bad." She spreads the fabric smooth. "We need to get Doc Talbot out here." She casts a glance at her husband, and he grimaces. "Nothin' we can do."

7

Doc Talbot sways in the driver's seat as the carriage stops at the front of the Goodnight house. Sitting unsteadily, he stares through round spectacles toward the two-story clapboard structure, removes his leather bowler, and wipes greasy black hair back with a hand. Lowering his palm to his stubbly cheek, he continues staring with weary incomprehension. He pulls a bottle of morphine from the pocket of his overcoat, removes the cork, and sips from it to feel the medicine, thick on his tongue. Swallowing hard, he allows his vision to go blurry.

"Doctor Talbot." Mr. Goodnight approaches the wagon.

The doctor blinks and shakes his head a bit. He hurries to close the bottle and put it in his pocket. "Yes, yes. Let's get to it." Turning, he reaches into the back of the wagon to retrieve a wooden case. It is similar in size and shape to a case that an established family would use to store its silver flatware. He holds it by a handle and steps cautiously from the wagon. "Carry my bag, would you? It's there on the seat."

Mr. Goodnight retrieves the black leather bag and takes Doc Talbot by the elbow to lead him up the steps onto the porch.

At the door to the sickroom, Doc Talbot smells the pus and knows the severity of the infection. As a Union Army doctor he had seen many such cases. For an instant, his mind flashes back to a soldier whose thigh had become terribly infected following a confederate officer's sword thrust. He recalls hacking at the boy's leg and sees, in a hazy vision, the chunks of flesh hanging in the teeth of his saw.

Mr. Goodnight opens the door to the sickroom, and the surgeon steps through it to see Horace.

"Let's see your hand, son." The doctor notices Horace grimace as he lifts his arm and sees the desperation in his eyes.

"Have a swig." He pulls the cork and hands him the bottle of morphine.

Horace drinks, and the doctor studies his swollen hand.

"It's gotta come off."

"Can't you save it?" Mrs. Goodnight raises her brows.

"The infection's too far gone. The bone. It's in the bone." He turns away swiftly and removes his overcoat. "Give him some booze, then bring him out to the porch. Light's better there. Bring some cloths and a candle."

The Goodnights look at each other and then to Horace.

"Don't let him." He looks to Mrs. Goodnight. "Don't let him cut off my hand." Tears flow down his cheeks. "Please."

"Calm down, dear." She pats his thigh. "We have no choice." She looks him tenderly in the eye. "I'll get you a drink."

She reaches for the bottle, but he beats her to it.

8

"Okay, lay him here." Doc Talbot kneels on a step next to his open case of surgical tools and a burning candle.

The Goodnights lead Horace, who stumbles through the front door and to the top of the steps. They help him lay down upon the pine boards of the porch.

"That'll do." He takes an instrument from the velvet-lined case. A steel rod about ten inches long. The business end is a flat section, resembling a rounded blade. The other end is a wooden handle. The doctor gives Mrs. Goodnight the instrument. "Heat this cauter."

The doctor puts a loop of canvas over Horace's hand, slides it up his forearm, and pulls it tight. Cranking a knob, he cinches the strap to cut off the flow of blood to the hand. He gives Mr. Goodnight a cloth soaked in chloroform. "We're about to begin. Put this over his nose and mouth. Hold him steady while I cut."

Mr. Goodnight follows the directions. Horace's breathing slows, and his body loosens.

Doc Talbot removes a scalpel from his kit, looks at his reflection in it, and turns his attention to Horace's hand. He cuts into the pinky side of the arm, watches the reflective blade sink into the flesh just below the wrist. He slides the scalpel blade toward the knuckles, cutting just the skin, to a point halfway up the back of his hand. Then, he curves the blade smoothly across the back of the hand and down the thumb side. Behind the blade, blood and pus seep from the cut and flow between Horace's fingers. Turning the hand over, Doc Talbot slices across the inside of the wrist to complete the loop of the initial incision.

He turns Horace's hand back over and takes the cut edge of skin between his finger and thumb. Pulling on the flap of skin, the doctor peels it toward the elbow. He hears the familiar, sloppy sound. Like opening the cover of a book, he lays back the skin to reveal red tissue, tendons, and wrist bones.

Mrs. Goodnight drops the cauter, and it clangs against the wood.

"Hold steady, misses. We've just begun."

He sets the scalpel to the side and removes a metacarpal saw from the kit. It has a tapering blade about five inches long with fine triangular teeth. He takes the black ebony handle firmly in hand, holds Horace's forearm so that his thumb points up, and rests the saw blade on the large tendon, crossing the radius and scaphoid bones.

He thrusts the blade forward to slice through the tendon, and Horace's thumb falls limp. The blade shreds an artery, and blood drips from it. The surgeon saws deliberately, feeling the handle twist slightly in his hand, as the narrow blade guides itself through the curving joint between hand and lower arm bones.

Doc Talbot grimaces when he feels the saw bind between the bones. Pressing his lips tightly together, he increases his force to grind the jagged teeth of the saw along the ends of the bones. As he saws, the doctor listens to the sound of the saw cutting through Horace's flesh. It reminds him of cutting fire wood. His mind begins to drift, but he is brought back to the present when he notices Horace's face twitch. The doctor stops and stares at the boy's face to see his eyes stir.

"The chloroform!" Doc Talbot nods. "Get the chloroform!"

Horace's eyes, bloodshot and dilated, spring open. He looks up at the midday sun. His chest rises with a gasping breath. His eyes to the right to see Doc Talbot, staring with eyebrows raised. His heart thumps, and he hears the pounding as though each heart beat were a gunshot. Pain pulses up his arm, but he refuses to look at it. He bites his lip hard and knits his brows, as he shifts his eyes from the doctor to Mr. Goodnight.

"Misses." The doctor shakes Mrs. Goodnight's shoulder. "The chloroform."

With trepidation, Horace looks down his right arm to see his hand with the saw hanging out of his wrist. Energy rushes through his limbs, the corners of his mouth pull back, and he cuts loose with a long, agonized, animal howl. The muscles in the front of his body contract, and he bucks against the restraining hands of Mr. Goodnight and Doc Talbot. His bare feet thrash against the wooden boards.

Panting, he tries to roll to his right, but the rancher constrains him. He squirms and kicks and, rolling to his left, overcomes Doc Talbot's restraining grasp. He wrenches his arm free from his grip. The saw falls from his wrist to the porch. When it hits the boards, it produces a ringing, springy sound.

He struggles with Mr. Goodnight, reaches out with his right arm and sees the cut drip blood onto the rancher. Horace struggles to his feet, looks left and right, and staggers toward the end of the porch. He quickly loses energy and has to lean against the house. "My hand." He collapses to the porch.

"Misses." The doctor raises his eyebrows. "The chloroform." Looking into her terrified eyes, the surgeon bites his lip.

After relocating, Doctor Talbot takes the saw from the porch and wipes it with a cloth. He slides the blade through the cut until he meets resistance. Flashing his eyes toward Mr. Goodnight, he resumes cutting.

One by one, Horace's fingers curl loosely, and blood spills from the gap. His hand hangs down from its own weight, and, when Doc Talbot saws through the last tendon, it flops onto the porch. The last bit of blood drains from it to soak into the yellow wood.

The Doctor sets the saw aside and pats the stump dry with a cloth. He removes bone dust from the stump with a stiff brush and takes another tool from the kit. This one resembles a fisherman's gaff. It is a hook on a handle. He digs the tip of the hook into an artery and pulls it out a bit. "Hold this."

Mr. Goodnight takes the handle in his hand, and the surgeon quickly ties off the artery. They repeat this procedure for each severed blood vessel, then the doctor gestures for Mrs. Goodnight to hand him the cauter. She removes the blade from the flame and hands him the instrument. He takes it quickly and applies the red-hot blade to every exposed surface of the stump. The tissues sizzle, and the scent of burning flesh rises in a wisp of foul smoke.

9

Days pass in a blur of pain and hazy morphine visions of Helen.

In the dark of night, she comes to him. She hovers over him like a cloud of cigarette smoke. The flowing, roiling vapor shifts forms, assumes shape after shape until she appears as the woman he had seen by Asa's side. In this form, she runs her hands through his hair and caresses his cheek with her fingertips. Then, she descends to him. She joins him in bed to press against him, wrap herself around him, and slowly writhe against him. She pours herself over him like molten chocolate over a strawberry and whispers into his ear. He reaches out to embrace her but finds only a wool blanket.

On the third morning after the amputation, Mrs. Goodnight arrives with beef steak and fried eggs. Horace sits up, and she feeds him. Bite after bite, she satisfies his hunger, and his strength grows until he is eager to leave the sickroom.

Mr. Goodnight stops by to see him much improved. "We'll drive out to the canyon." He looks Horace in the eyes. "Say goodbye to J.C."

Mr. Goodnight drives the covered wagon through the herd of cattle, scattered across the tall yellow grass. He heads east toward Jackrabbit Canyon. Mrs. Goodnight rides by his side. In the back, the frozen body of J.C. Garcia rocks stiffly, and Horace rides by its side.

Resting his bandaged stump on J.C.'s forehead, Horace listens to the cattle's low, slow, inarticulate mooing as it stretches through time and space. The mournful sound pulls at him until his heart seems to vibrate in sympathy with it, and tears flow down his cheeks to splash J.C.'s face.

Images of the vaquero's eyes shine in his imagination like the full moon in the night sky, and Horace addresses him. "What will I do, J.C.? What will I do without you?" He reaches out with his left hand, places it on J.C.'s frozen cheek, and feels the still emptiness of death. "How will I become a man like you and my father?"

At the mouth of the canyon, near a dry creek bed, Mr. Goodnight stops the wagon. He and Mrs. Goodnight climb down and walk to the back. He pulls the shovel from the bed of the wagon. "You stay."

Horace nods and presses his lips together. He looks down at the stiff face of J.C. Garcia, notices the familiar, bent nose and stubbly jaw, but he longs to look into his shining hazel eyes. He wishes the eyes would open to reveal their lively light but knows that will not happen.

He listens to the sound of Mr. Goodnight's shovel, cutting through the dense soil, and his heart slows to match the steady rhythm. The scent of freshly-turned earth reaches him, and the finality of his friend's death settles upon him.

Dirt piles up at the sides of the grave, and Mr. Goodnight continues digging. His determination to give the man a decent burial drives him to dig deeper, and he slowly descends into the cold earth as the hole deepens.

Three feet.

Four feet.

As the sun settles beyond the Medicine Bow Mountains, an exhausted Mr. Goodnight climbs from the grave, thrusts the shovel into the ground for the last time, and gestures for Horace, who struggles from the bed of the wagon and walks to his side.

"Help me with the body."

Horace turns back to the wagon to see J.C. beneath the canopy.

"Take a foot."

He reaches out with his left hand and grasps the back side of J.C.'s right foot. Mr. Goodnight takes the left, and the two pull. The stiff body slowly slides, scuffing against the rough wood, until it extends stiffly from the end of the wagon, and they let the feet down so that it leans. They stand and take hold of the arms and, rotating the corpse slightly, lay it next to the hole.

They kneel at the ends of the body and slide it toward the grave. When they have the corpse teetering on the edge, Horace looks upon J.C.'s face, smeared with his own blood and tears. He looks into the dark hole, and his mind reels with images of J.C. and his father resting there. His stomach churns, and the blood drains from his face. Dizziness overcomes him as the gravity of death reaches out to him, beckons him. In a fearful moment, he pushes the body of J.C. Garcia over the edge into the grave.

The corpse takes only a split second to reach the bottom, but Horace experiences in that moment the collapse of his world. A long, slow breath escapes his lips, and the smiling face of Asa Moyer rises in his awareness.

Hatred fills his heart. Hatred of that man burns in him like an ember glowing in ashes.

His body quakes as he pushes dirt onto J.C.'s corpse then stands beneath the vast, star-speckled sky.

"J.C. Garcia was a second father to me." Tears flow down Horace's smooth cheeks. "He was a good man. A good friend to myself and my father." He swallows hard. "He was a cowboy from Texas. Gunned down in Wyoming." A grim

expression comes over his face. "And I will avenge his death."
He grits his teeth. "I will kill Asa Moyer."

10

As Horace declares his intention to avenge J.C.'s murder and his own maiming, a lone figure approaches from the west. The silhouette stumbles across the moonlit prairie toward the burial party. Horace and the Goodnights watch the man approach, and Mr. Goodnight goes to the front of the wagon to retrieve his rifle. He racks the lever on the yellow boy to chamber a round and levels the barrel toward the man.

"Don't shoot." The man approaches the wagon. "Don't shoot."

Mr. Goodnight trains his sights on him, notices his salt and pepper beard and the blood stains on the chest and sleeve of his white shirt.

The man stands with his hands held away from his sides. "Ma name's Domino. Domino Lanham."

"What ya doin' on my property?"

"Can't say as I know. Kinda lost."

Where's yer horse?"

"Back in Laramie, I guess. Don't know for sure. I been shot."

"Who done it?"

"The marshal done it. Bloody Steve shot me and laughed."

"Why?"

"Cheatin' at cards." Domino's voice cracks. "I'm a no good cheat."

Mr. Goodnight looks into his eyes and feels the weight of his rifle. "You hurt bad?"

"It'll heal fast, but I been wanderin' 'cross the grass for a while. I'm tired and hungry." Domino gives Mr. Goodnight a pleading expression. "Got no family. No place to go."

Mr. Goodnight studies him by the pale moonlight. He thinks of the injured man wandering the prairie and secretly admires his perseverance.

"Just lost a good man. Can you swing a hammer? Shoot a gun?"

"Ta tell the truth, I'm no good at work."

"What good are you?"

Domino shifts his eyes to the side. "I'm a schemer."

Mr. Goodnight licks his lips. "Con man?" The old man lowers his gun. "Might could use a good schemer. You aint scammin' me now are ya, boy?"

"Lord no. Look here at my shoulder all bloody."

Mr. Goodnight steps up to the man and draws close to peer through the hole in his shirt. He pokes a finger through it, presses his fingertip against Domino's shoulder until he feels the wound, scabbed over. He removes his finger from the hole, looks Domino in the eye briefly, and jerks a thumb over his shoulder. "Ride in the back with the boy."

Everyone boards the wagon, Mr. Goodnight works the reins, and the horse begins pulling the wagon so that it arcs across the grass back toward the ranch house. Horace glances at Domino, who flashes him a close-lipped smile.

"Friend of yourn?"

Horace looks at the stranger. "Yeah."

"Sorry." Domino presses his lips together and nods. Glancing at Horace, he sees the boy's inconsolable sullenness and unsatisfied anger. "Lost a brother back in Louisville." Looking down, Domino speaks deliberately. "He was a rambler and a smart ass. Travelled all around the south. Went from town to town doin' shit kicker jobs 'till his mouth got 'im in trouble. Then he'd go to the next town for a while, do some work and lay 'round with some whore or 'nother. That was him. Fun-lovin layabout. Never meant no harm, but he had a sass mouth and couldn't take direction much. Anyway, he was stayin' in Louisville. Third floor of a place. Musta pissed off the locals." Domino licks his lips and flashes his eyes to the side. "Dern fools killed 'im. Threw 'im from the window." He forces a slight smile. "An' I had to bury my brother in a strange city, away from our mountain home." He falls silent and rubs his hands together.

Horace wipes his eye and clears his throat. "What'd ya do?"

Domino looks at Horace and feels the drift of his mind. "I waited." He bites the tip of his tongue. "I waited 'til I caught each one of 'em alone." He nods. "An' I killed 'em. One by one, I killed 'em all. Left 'em lying in their own blood."

"Will you help me?" Horace raises his brows. "Ride with me?"

"Who done it?"

"Moyer's gang."

"Took your hand too?"

"Yeah."

Domino leans his head back a bit and casts his eyes up to the canopy. "Them rebs is outta hand. Power mad an' blood lusty." He nods. "Gotta be done the right way. Gotta outsmart 'em." He blinks. "Yeah." The schemer looks Horace in the eyes. "I'll help ya."

11

"First things first." Domino smiles and casts a glance about the interior of the bunkhouse. "Ya gettin' a hook?"

"Doc's gonna bring it."

"Good." Domino nods. "Shoot leftie?"

"Never tried."

"Time ta learn."

"Got no gun, well, maybe." He falls silent.

"Maybe what?"

"J.C. had a Griswold." Horace licks his lips. "It was my father's."

"Where is it?"

"The misses has it." Horace lowers his eyes. "Gotta get that gun."

"What's gonna convince her to give it to ya?"

"Revenge?"

"Women don't work like that."

"Love? But she wasn't close to J.C."

"An' you? Does she love you?"

"Yeah. Treats me special like I was her own."

"I see it, but she won't want you chasin' damnation. You'll never get your father's gun that way. You gotta appeal to her interest. What does she have to lose?"

"The Moyer gang is after the ranch. Gonna run the Goodnights off or kill 'em. Aint no one here to protect 'em 'cept me and you. The old man's strong, but he can't fight 'em by himself. He needs our help."

"That's why he lets me stay." Domino nods. "He needs me."

"Yeah. Let's go to her. Get my gun and one for--"

"No." Domino interrupts. "We go to him."

"But she has it."

"The old man calls the shots." Domino nods. "We'll go to him. Won't be hard to get his backin'. He arms us. We take out the Moyer gang. He gets to keep the ranch. All ends well."

"Not all that simple." Horace swallows. "They got a woman." He rubs his face. "Keep her in a cage. All locked up like some circus beast. And there's another. Name's Helen. Friend of Asa's." He shakes his head. "I don't know." He shrugs. "She has some kinda hold on me. Comes in my dreams."

"Makes love to you?"

"Yeah."

Domino sighs. "She's not human." He looks Horace in the eyes. "She's a demon from hell."

Horace's face flushes. "How do you know?"

"Probably led Asa to power." But now she's done with him. He can't give her what she wants."

"How do you know?"

"I have some knowledge of such things. I was once a travelling preacher. Well, I pretended to be. Besides, she comes to me, too. Ever since I been here, she's been callin' my name, runnin' her hands through her dark hair, and offerin' herself." He presses his lips together. "Seems she needs a new fool."

"Yeah."

"And we have a powerful foe."

Horace swallows hard.

"You'll have to be strong." He nods. "Best say a --"

Gunfire interrupts Domino, and the two rush to the small window of the bunkhouse to peer through it. They see three riders wearing Confederate Army hats. The men ride left and right in tight, nervous maneuvers and fire their weapons into the air. Horace sees their cold breath rise foggy in the air to mix with gun smoke and hears one of them call out. "Old man!" He fires again. "You have tomorrow to pack up and move on." The confederates turn and ride back toward town. Horace looks toward the main house to see Mr. Goodnight at a window.

"Seems the clock is tickin'." Domino looks at Horace.

As the sun settles, and its last rays brush gently across the blood-stained porch, the men meet to discuss the ultimatum.

"Aint goin nowhere." Mr. Goodnight declares. "This is our place, and we aint gonna leave it for some mangy rebs."

"Okay, then," Domino says, "what we gonna do?"

"We're gonna fight." The old man spits. "We're gonna stand here and fight for all we're worth. Hope you are with me on this, Domino."

"Don't take too kindly to what them boys is tryin' ta do." He rubs his face. "Yeah. I'm in."

12

Doc slides the leather harness over Horace's stump, pulls it up his forearm, and cinches it tight with the leather laces. Horace looks down the length of his forearm to see the crisscrossing laces and, at the end, where his hand once was, a grey metal hook, satiny in the morning sun.

"This should help ya get along." Doc smiles.

Horace nods as he turns the hook about before him to study it from various angles.

"Just don't pet no dogs or scratch your face." Doc laughs. "And don't sleep with it on."

Horace smiles.

"I'm sure glad you made it. Things were iffy for a bit."

"Yeah." Horace looks him in the eyes. "Thanks, Doc."

"Take care."

Doc walks through the door of the bunkhouse, boards his wagon, and pulls off toward town.

Horace looks to Domino with wide, bright eyes. "I have an idea."

"What's that?"

"You'll see when I'm done." Horace smiles. "You wanna talk to the old man? Get the Griswold and somethin' for you."

Domino looks at Horace, studying the hook. A slight smile spreads across his face. He walks through the door and heads toward the house.

Horace reaches under his bunk and retrieves a wooden case. He lifts the lid and rummages around until he finds what he's looking for. "This should do the trick."

"Don't want the boy runnin' off on some fool quest for vengeance." Mr. Goodnight looks sternly at Domino. "Them rebs is ornery folk. Not gonna stand still for ya."

"I know. Ya seen what they done ta me. Shot me. Robbed me. Left me for the mountain lions, and they're comin for ya." He takes a deep breath. "Comin' ta take yer land. Yer home. And they don't care what it takes ta get it."

"The boy's father was a good man. Stood his ground 'gainst injuns when he had to. Lost his life pushin' cattle up here to me." Mr. Goodnight presses his lips together. "Feel responsible for the boy now that J.C. is gone, and, dern it, I don't want him rushin' into no rebel meat grinder." Mr. Goodnight clamps his teeth together.

"I fought with them boys. Confederates. Weren't much good at soldierin', but I done it, and I know how they think." Domino blinks. "They done sent riders out ta scare us." He looks at Mr. Goodnight with wide eyes. "Next they'll come with torches to burn us out. You're right, we gotta stand up to 'em. But, after that, we gotta take the fight inta town. Kill 'em all and free the woman. We gotta take back the town." Domino presses his lips together. "Just so happens that me and the boy got good reason ta do it."

"Recon you're right." The old man bites his lip. "Least I can do is give the boy his gun."

"And me? Ya got one for me?"

Mr. Goodnight takes a deep breath and lets it rush out. "Yeah. Got a couple Dragoons. I'm keepin' my yella boy." He half smiles. "You can ride Stella."

Arms loaded with weapons and ammunition, Domino pushes the bunkhouse door with his foot. It glides open to reveal Horace working at a small wooden table. He continues for a brief moment, and Domino recognizes the sound produced by his work. It is a file moving across metal. He realizes what Horace is up to, and his face lights up with joy.

Horace looks up and sees Domino's thrilled expression. He smiles and raises the hook to show him. Candlelight glints off the fine tip and sharpened edge of the hook. He swings it left and right like a sword and thrusts the tip into a wooden tabletop. It penetrates an inch or so, and he pries it to tear a chunk of wood from the table.

Domino laughs. "That's damn fine, Horace." He shakes his head. "Damn fine. You'll really do some damage with that."

"That Asa's gonna wish he never seen me."

"Make 'im pay." Domino grins. "With blood."

"Yeah." Horace's lip twitches.

13

"See ya got the Griswold."

Domino sets the load on his bunk and picks up the long-barreled pistol. He shakes it a couple times to feel its heft. "These things sure do pack a wallop." He studies the side of it. "Carried one in the war."

"You fought in the war?" Horace blurts it out with childish excitement.

"Fought with John Bell Hood. Saw action in Nashville and continued with him until they sent me to serve guard duty at Andersonville." He looks seriously at Horace. "You heard of Andersonville aint ya?"

Horace shakes his head no.

"Well it really put the lie to ideas of Southern decency and culture. Horrible. Just horrible, what they done ta them poor boys. I'd heard the rumors 'bout starvation, but those were just rumors. Then I saw for myself. Them boys wastin' away into pathetic wisps of skin and bone. Lookin' at me with bulgin' eyes and beggin' for scraps. It was bad. I'd never imagined that kind of sufferin'." He looks again at Horace. "I couldn't stand it and had to get outta there, so I left."

"You just left? Simple as that?"

"Weren't simple. When you're Army property, you don't just come and go as you please. I had to escape."

"How'd ya do it?"

"Well, I gathered up my weapons and ammo, then I waited for a really dark night and snuck up to the outside fence. There was a guard there, posted up in a high shack. Some fella I didn't much know. He was stern. Career Army. I crept up under his lookout post and waited for the chance to climb the fence. It was a tall stockade. At least fifteen feet. Anyway, I stood under his pigeon roost and against the fence and waited.

Nothin' happened for a long time, and I kept on waitin'. Still nothin' happened, so I pulled a brass button from my jacket and tossed it hard against a nearby tent. It rattled 'round a bit and that fella called out, 'Halt!'" Domino smiles. "When he hollered, I tossed a rope over the fence and scampered up and over quicker than owls shit."

"He didn't see ya?"

"Guess not. Nobody shot or shouted."

"But they missed ya the next day."

"Sure, but by then I was deep in the Georgia woods and headin' east for the coast. Would've been shorter to cut north into Tennessee, but I'd have run inta plenty of soldiers, so I kinda tried to duck and dodge through the pines. After a while, I realized the forest was deserted. Not a human soul for miles, and I was lost. I knew the coast was to the east, so each mornin' I set myself walking toward the sun.

"Then one mornin' I heard a scamperin' in the woods, and I stood real quiet, and there came another rustle in the trees, and the birds flew off sudden like. I stood still, fearin' some soldiers had found me. Thought they were gonna take me back, but I'd be a prisoner this time, and I'd have to drink that shit-filled creek water and fight for my meagre rations. So I stood real still and silent. Didn't twitch a muscle, as the sunlight winnowed through the thick pines. Then there came another sound. Low and beastlike. I raised my Griswold slow. I could hear my breath, fitful, as I stared down the barrel toward the spot where I heard the sound and I waited for the soldiers to step out. Just stood there tryin' to breathe, 'til the tension got to be too much, and I had to force a confrontation, so I stepped slowly forward. Just as my foot landed on the dried pine, he burst out at me, low and vicious, squeelin' like he come squirtin' up from the depths of Hell. A wild boar with great huge tusks. He came chargin' right at me, and before I could aim and fire, he gouged my thigh. I dropped the pistol and fell bleedin' to the ground. I heard him snort again and struggled to my feet. I scampered off a bit and heard him after me, followin' me. Looked 'round but couldn't see him. But I heard him snortin' low.

"Damn pig followed me day after day, spooked off any squirrel or rabbit I was aimin' to kill, and pushed me, tired and hungry, through that forest and into the Okefenokee Swamp, where I finally got the better of him.

"One night I cut a long oak limb and sharpened one end of it and hardened it in my small fire. Then I climbed an oak tree and waited. Sure enough, the sun came up and that old bore got mighty bothered when he couldn't find me. He started snortin and diggin' 'round in the dirt. And he squealed out long and angry like. Then he came sniffin' 'round my camp spot 'til he wandered right under me. I dropped down from the tree with that spear held down, and I ran him through with it. Damn thing squealed and thrashed about and jolted, but I'd run the spear into the ground, and he couldn't do nothin' but run on the spot 'til he died.

"I laid him out and butchered him good and proper. Then I skewered his heart and cooked it over a fire and ate it. Tasty, tender vittles. After savourin' my victory, I looked 'round to see that I was surrounded by gators, all eyes bulgin' from the water headed my way. I tossed the chunks of meat to 'em and ran off 'til I found a river flowin' east. Found out later, it was the St. Mary. Followed it to the coast.

"When I got there, I boarded a black market cotton transport that took me into New England. Along the way, I traded my Confederate Army gear for the clothes of a clergyman. When I arrived, got me a mule and a wagon and set off to spread the Word. I knew enough about the Lord to pass as a travelling preacher. That's how I made it back home to Ithica. But when I got home, I found another man tending my garden and courtin' my wife.

"I rolled into Ithica dressed as a preacher and set up my little tent for revival. Seems the whole town turned out, and no one recognized me. I planned to preach on forgiveness, but damned if that fella didn't waltz straight into my tent lookin' right cozy with my Penelope, and I changed my topic to God's wrath. I aim ta tell ya, Horace, my blood boiled when I saw him 'n' her together. I saw red, but I maintained my disguise, kept preachin' from the pulpit. All the time, I'm lookin' out at 'em together.

"I had to know if she still loved me. Had she given me up for dead? Was he forcing himself on her? Well, I soon found out. As is the custom 'round home, travellin' preachers are honored guests, and guess who offered. My Penelope. Of course, I accepted her invite, and that evenin' after services, I rode 'round to be a guest in my own home.

"We had tomatoes that fella had grown in my garden and her fabulous lamb, golden brown and juicy, just as I remembered. I sat at my table, wonderin' why she didn't recognize me. Had the war changed me so much? Had she forgotten my face?

"I looked into her eyes and felt my love for her. I had come this far to see her. Her image had kept me going through the hard times, but to her I was a stranger. My heart wept, but I kept it under wraps. I had to know. Did she still love me? So I says, "That was a fine meal Mrs.--" and he stepped in with "Miss Keene." I saw her eyes start to glisten with tears, and I had my answer. I wanted to rise up then and there. I wanted to rise up in fury and righteous indignation to slay him with my bare hands. I imagined his blood splashing across his smug expression and his eyes going blank. But I thought of her and kept my rage in check. I would have to bide my time. Wait for the perfect opportunity.

"Then it came to me. I saw that the colossal fool carried my Colt 1860. I knew the sights were bent. So I proposed a shooting contest. The winner would have the honor of dancing with the lady of the house. He stammered a bit, but I jibbed him and he agreed.

"The first shot was his. An empty bottle set on a stump served as a target. He drew the Colt and aimed carefully. I watched nervously. Had he figured out the workin' of my pistol? Had he indeed taken my place? I bit my lower lip and waited as he leveled the barrel toward the bottle and squeezed the trigger. Boom!

"He missed!

"My heart danced. It spun 'round in my chest like some dancehall girl spinnin' as the piano played. Skirts all ruffelin'. I felt the blood rush to my face. And the poor fool shook his head, when he handed me the pistol. 'Here ya go, brother.'

"I took it comfortable in my hand, and a flood of memories raced through my mind. We had built this house and lived happy in it until the war started and they came callin' for me. That started my wanderin'. But now I was home. I kneaded the grip in my palm and aimed high and right. I licked my lips and squeezed the trigger. Boom!

"An explosion of shattered glass filled my vision, and in that moment she knew me for her husband, home from the war. Tears flowed from her eyes, and she ran to me. I took her into my arms and held her, and that damned fool's mouth hung open just enough for me to shove the tip of my gun into it.

"He stared up at me, and I felt the curved trigger beneath my finger. I waited. Held that barrel in his mouth and waited. Just as I was about to let him go, he jumped up, grabbed the pistol in his hands and we set to scrappin'. He was getting' the better of me, then the gun went off, and we both fell still as poor Penelope clutched her chest and collapsed to the ground, blood soaking her fine church dress.

"I rushed to her. Felt her last breath upon my cheek. When I'd buried her and finished weepin', I tracked 'im down and killed 'im. I slit his throat and burned his body, and set off wanderin' again."

Horace looks into Domino's wistful eyes. He feels the man's suffering but doubts his sanity and the full authenticity of his tale.

14

Looking down the shaking 8-inch barrel of the Griswold, Horace tries to line up the sights. Down range stands a tree stump, his intended target. The muzzle rises and falls with the twitching of his hand, and his foggy breath obscures his vision to make the task still more difficult. As the front sight wavers around the target, Horace recalls his father's training and says quietly, "Squeeze the trigger. Don't jerk or pull. Just squeeee--" Boom! The pistol bucks and rises in his hand, and a cloud of grey smoke obscures his vision. He runs to the stump to inspect it for damage.

"You missed." Domino calls out after him. "To the right."

Kneeling at the stump, Horace checks for signs of impact.

"Come on back."

He rises to his feet and walks back toward Domino.

"Ya need strength in yer arm and hand. Go split some wood."

"With one hand?"

"That should do it." He nods. "I'm gonna scout about, look for a spot to ambush them rebs."

"Aint no tree to hide behind." Horace chuckles. "No rock neither."

"I was thinkin' we could walk out and lay low with our guns." Domino rubs his jaw. "Surprise 'em."

"Might be waitin' a long time." Horace grins.

Domino's face burns with rising anger. "Don't hear no choppin'."

"Aint gonna be none."

"You wanna get strong, don't ya?"

"Yeah, but—"

"Suit yerself." Domino presses his lips together and rubs his forehead as he focuses on Horace's face. "Yer growin' a beard."

"Yeah."

Looking at him, Domino smiles. "Looks good." He shakes his head a little. "Looks damn good. How 'bout we check out the lay of the land. See what we have to work with."

As darkness settles across the high plains, Horace and Domino survey the grounds and determine the confederates will most likely take the passage between the bunkhouse and the shed toward the main house. This is where they will make their stand. They study the area, and Horace gets an idea. "We got some lamp oil."

"Yeah?" Domino's eyelids settle and he cocks his head to the side.

"And a tarp." A sly smile spreads across Horace's face, and his eyes light up. "Alright. Let's make a trap. Burn those bastards."

They gather together the materials and set to work. Domino soaks a canvas tarp with fuel oil and spreads it out between the two buildings. They cover over the tarp with dry grass to camouflage it, and it blends quite well with the surroundings. Horace mounts a long board to the side wall of the bunkhouse with a hinge and connects a large spring to it, while Domino strings a tripwire across the fuel-soaked tarp toward the board. Everything comes together, and all that remains is to clean their guns and wait for the confederates to arrive.

The night before a battle is either a drunken or restless affair. This is one of those dreadful nights, filled with worry and anxious tossing on uncomfortable bunks. When Horace finally drifts off, his sleep is disturbed by dreams of his father and J.C. and Helen."

She comes to him, lovely in her nakedness, turning and gyrating, soothing his fear. She bends over him to kiss his forehead, and he wakes to find Domino looking out the window.

"She come to ya?"

Horace looks at him.

"Kiss ya on the forehead?"

"Yeah."

15

As the sun nears the horizon, Horace and Domino peer anxiously through the side window of the bunkhouse. Their weapons are clean and loaded, and all is in order with the fire trap. They scan the horizon and wait for the confederates to appear. Not a word passes between them as they watch. Then, from around the corner of the shed, the shadow of the mounted rebs creeps across the ground.

The two flash wide-eyed expressions to one another and spring into action. Horace grabs his small torch, ducks below the window sill and fumbles with his matches. He lights the torch. Meanwhile, Domino slips through the door and moves stealthily to the end of the bunkhouse.

Horace peers through a slit in the heavy curtains to see them enter the passage. He hears their gear rattle with each pace and holds tight as the lead horse walks into the wire. The wire stretches a bit then pulls the lynch pin to set off the spring-loaded arm with a bucket of lamp oil attached to the top of it. The arm swings down to splash the kerosene on the riders. The horses rear up, and Horace throws the lit torch through the window onto the fuel-soaked tarp. It ignites a fireball, and the horses catch fire. The horses scream and buck and bolt off, throwing one rider to the burning tarp. He catches fire and rolls about in the flames. Horace runs through the door and watches from the corner of the bunkhouse as the second man rides his burning horse into the night.

Through the hazy smoke of burning flesh, Horace sees the third rider about thirty feet away. He watches the confederate reach into his saddle bag to pull out a torch. The reb lights it, and his horse snorts and tries to turn away, but the rider checks him and urges him forward. Slowly, the rebel approaches, torch raised, red-orange fire raging at the end.

Horace steps out from behind the bunkhouse and squares off against him. The rider continues his slow approach toward the dying flames, and Horace draws his father's Griswold. He sees the glare from the torch and, by its fierce light, the reb's brass buttons and scowling face.

Horace raises the pistol toward the approaching man. His hand shakes violently, and he struggles to draw a breath. He tries to fire, but his finger will not respond. Squeeze the trigger, Horace. Nothing. The confederate nears. Horace hears him laugh quietly. Squeeze the trigger. Images of his father and J.C. rise up in his imagination. Visions of the two men riding headlong into the attacking Comanche fill Horace with ambition and moxie. As the mounted rebel rides to within five feet, Horace, raising the pistol high above his shoulder, stands his ground. He feels the heat from the flame and the glare from it plays havoc with his vision. His hand shakes, and he draws a quivering breath through clinched teeth. Damn it, Horace, squeeze the tri—Boom!

The Confederate jolts back, and a spray of blood douses Horace's cheek. The reb drops the torch as his horse rears up, turns, and rushes toward the darkness. Gradually the rider falls from the saddle, and Horace looks at the pistol in his hand. It is not smoking. He turns his head across his shoulder to see a smiling Mr. Goodnight at a window of the main house. Moonlight shines through gun smoke and glints off the brass of his yellow boy.

Horace lets out a sudden breath, and a tear flows down his cheek, as Domino runs, hooting and hollering, toward him. He slaps Horace on the back. "Way ta stand yer ground."

"Yeah, but--"

"But nothin'."

Mr. and Mrs. Goodnight join the celebration, and, for a moment, the moon seems to shine a bit brighter in the night sky.

16

One horse survives. One smoldering horse struggles back into town and makes his way to the livery stable. The stable hand recognizes the poor creature as Georgia Jim's charger. A shiver runs along his spine, and he knows the situation in Laramie is about to get out of hand. He runs to the "Belle" to spread the word.

"You're shittin' me, boy." Bloody Steve peers down on the young man with his one eye.

"Naw, sir. He come limpin' into the stable all smokin' and sizzlin'. Been burned powerful bad."

Bloody Steve's lips pull back to expose his yellow teeth, and his eyebrow presses heavily upon his eye. He draws a breath through his stained teeth. "That boy's gonna pay fer this."

"We got no time to lose. Gotta strike fast. Ride fer town tonight." Domino thrusts his fist into his palm. "Them bastards won't know what hit 'em."

"I'll get the horses." Horace rushes off to the shed, where Mrs. Goodnight approaches him.

"Horace." Her voice is soft and sweet. "Honey."

"Yessum."

"I want you to know we're proud of you."

Horace's heart shivers.

"And I know your momma and daddy would be proud of you, too." She lays her hand on his cheek. "And J.C."

Horace's stomach twitches, and he draws a spastic breath.

"He would be proud of you."

His chin quivers beneath the fine whiskers of his first beard.

"I want you to wear his spurs." She smiles kindly. "Let me put them on for you." She gestures for Horace to raise his booted foot. Horace loops his hook across a board to support himself, standing on one foot, and she straps the spurs to one heel then the other.

Leading Orville and Stella, Horace walks, spurs jingling, and caresses the handle of his father's Griswold. Tears stream down his face, and he feels the weight and responsibility, the bourdon of being a man in the Wild West.

The two men mount their horses.

Mr. Goodnight looks up to Horace. "What's yer plan?"

"Blood." Horace swallows hard. "Blood."

A glimmer of moonlight shines on the vast expanse of golden grass to light the way for Horace and Domino. The two men ride steadily along the freshly-laid tracks toward Laramie, glowing on the horizon. Horace looks at it, studies it, and recalls the first time he approached the town at night. He had been overcome by dread upon first seeing its ominous glow. The dull light had spoken of the lust and greed and hatred in man's dark heart, but now he sees it differently. He sees the hope and love and unconquerable spirit of a people and place, struggling for expression despite the confederate reign of terror. He presses his lips together, feels for his Griswold in its holster, and recalls the caged woman. He thinks of her tangled hair, hanging in golden strands across her eyes. He is bound for the "Belle of the West." He aims to kill Asa Moyer but realizes his true purpose is to free her and restore her majesty.

Guns drawn, Horace and Domino push through the front flaps of the "Belle" and cut through the rowdy crowd toward the back room. Sensing the impending shoot out, the revelers rush for the exits. Horace spots his dove, Justine, by the side door. He sees the fear and excitement in her eyes, as she backs up to the side wall and settles down to the floor.

He turns his attention to the curtain, the thin veil of concealment, separating the saloon from the working of infernal power behind. With fierce determination in his mind and rage in his heart, he steps toward it. Con Wager parts the curtains and steps through. His wide body makes an easy target for the steely-eyed Horace, who, without hesitation, squeezes off a round. The thunderous report of the Griswold fills the "Belle," and Horace's hand, held low by his hip, ratchets on his wrist to absorb the pistol's kick. The bullet strikes Con's left shoulder, and his body torques to that side. Horace strides forward. His spurs ring out in the hollow space of the "Belle," and he shoots again through the expanding cloud of black powder smoke. When the bullet blasts through his midsection, Con doubles over, clutches his left hand to his stomach, and staggers back. Blood seeps between his fingers, and he groans. His right hand reaches for the Colt at his side.

When Horace attempts to squeeze the trigger a third time a sudden rush of heat passes through his body. It is a moist heat that rises up from his feet to spread through his legs and torso and pass through his arms. Sweat beads form on his face, and his hand shakes. He struggles to hold the gun somewhat steady as Con fumbles with the string on his holster.

Horace raises the pistol, looks down the barrel toward the hunched figure before him. Squeeze the trigger, Horace. A high-pitched tone rings in his ears, but he doesn't merely hear it. The tone rings in him and through him. It seems to come from everywhere all at once. It rings in his mind and in his body. Gradually, all around him begins to fade to vaporous illusion. He stares down the barrel, as Con pulls his pistol from his holster. Squeeze the trigger. This time the thought has a different voice. It is a woman's voice, so soft and lilting sweet. As the world around him slowly dissolves into dream, Horace's arm shakes with the enormous effort to move his trigger finger. He draws a sharp breath, hissing through his teeth, and the gun fires. The bullet enters the top of Con's head, and the impact sends him toppling back to collapse on the pine boards. Blood spills from the wound, and gradually all sound fades to silence. Horace shakes his head and presses his eyes closed. He stands for a moment trying to recall his situation. The high-pitched tone rings in his awareness. Like a siren, it wails in a wavering, all-invasive assault on his being. He draws a long breath. Just as he lets the air pass through his parted lips, Bloody Steve, wielding two 1860's, pushes through the curtains.

The sudden movement startles Horace, and he drops to the floor. From behind, Domino manages to fire Mr. Goodnight's Colt. The bullet misses its mark, but sends Bloody Steve scurrying off to his right. Domino fires again and leaps over the bar on his right to take cover. Meanwhile Horace lay still on the pine boards.

From behind a toppled table, Bloody Steve fires at Horace, who hears the bullet zing past his head. Horace turns his eyes toward the opening in the curtain to see blue-eyed Helen, standing with her hands raised about shoulder high with her palms facing toward him. In front of her, at the blood-soaked pine table, sits Asa, unmoving.

Domino fires at Con. The bullet rips into the tabletop to shred the wood. Con fires back. Bottles shatter and liquor sprays through the air in a fine mist.

Horace stares at Helen, sees her lips twitch, as her face contorts into a grimace. His body aches. His joints pulse with pain and stiffen. The Griswold falls from his shaking hand, and his body begins to straighten. With great effort, he manages to roll to his right, toward the bar. Domino raises up to shoot again, but his pistol doesn't fire. He ducks behind the bar, reaches the pistol over the bar top to try it. Again it fails to shoot.

Seeing the situation, Bloody Steve takes aim at Horace, lying on the floor. A cruel smile stretches his Cyclops face, as he stares down the long barrel of the Dragoon. Just as Bloody Steve begins to squeeze the trigger, Domino heaves a whisky bottle toward him. The bottle crashes against the tabletop to send shards of glass into Bloody Steve's face and burning liquor into his eye. The shot goes wide of its mark but still hits Horace in the leg. The sharp pain wracks Horace, and he squeezes himself into a ball.

Domino tears a narrow post from the structure of the bar. He peers over the bar to see Bloody Steve, wiping the back of his hand across his eye. Domino glances at Horace, balled up on the floor, then leaps the bar and rushes across the saloon to crash into the overturned table, pinning Bloody Steve beneath it. Laying on the tabletop, Domino looks down into Bloody Steve's wide, blood-shot eye and puts the splintery end of the post up to it. The eye blinks hard, and Bloody Steve turns away, but Domino grabs him by the hair and turns his face toward him. When he looks again into the bully's face, Domino sees his chin quiver. He thrusts the post through his eye, shoves it deep into his skull. Blood spills from the cavity as Domino wallows the makeshift spear in his eye socket.

Horace struggles to his feet, hobbles to the curtain, and, with a wide swipe of his hook, pulls it down to reveal Asa, the caged Annabelle, and Helen, resplendent in beauty.

"Horace." She smiles. "You have proven yourself worthy."

Tears flow down Horace's face, as he approaches the table of suffering.

"Join us." She reaches out her hand.

He reaches out his hook, drags it across the rough, blood-stained wood.

"Laramie is just the beginning." She smiles. "Together we will rule the West."

From the corner of his eye, he sees the cage and Annabelle inside, now standing, dirty and disheveled but glistening with forgotten life and vitality.

He looks at Asa, slumping in his chair, mouth hanging open.

"Join us. Know the pleasure of my flesh."

He looks at her, scans her flawless figure.

"Anything you want."

"I want my hand back. I want J.C. back. You took these from me." He bites his lip. "Can't undo what's been done." He recalls his mother's last words, her wish that he live for love. He looks at Asa, a shell of a man, wasted away by his mad quest for power, drained by the demonic force of Helen. Pity rises in him to mix with the rage that had driven him to this point. Pressing his lips together, he extends the hook to his side. He glances at Helen, watching anxiously, and swings the hook in a large arc. When the tip of it strikes the side of Asa's head it passes through his temple to sink deep into his brain. Blood flows around the hook as Asa's body convulses and his dreams of infinite power dissolve into the reality of blood and pain and death.

Asa's body falls to the side, and Horace turns his eyes to Helen.

She smiles. "Now we can be together, just you and me."

"No." Horace's eyes narrow. "Now I will kill you."

"You fool." She laughs. "You can't kill me. I am forever."

Drawing the bloody prosthetic out to his side, he steps toward her and thrusts it deep into her gut. In a sparkling flash of blue light, the form of Helen dissolves, leaving only the satin dress, hanging from his hook. He stands in awe as the bright light moves through the air toward Justine, the raven-haired dove, and enters her body, which fades out of this realm of existence.

He stands silent for a long moment, then swallows hard and blinks as though clearing his mind after a strange dream. His eyes shift to the right, where he sees Annabelle. He gazes at her, and she says in a voice so soft and lilting sweet, "my hero."

His heart thrills, and he limps to the cage to free her.

Justine

On the small stage in the back room of Phoenix Hill Tavern, David Guiot strides toward the overhead spotlight. He leans back into the smoky white beam and casts his eyes up into the light. His pupils constrict, and sweat seeps from his forehead.

He strikes a wailing note on his candy red, electric guitar, and makes the tone whine and whimper against the driving base beat. Gradually, he raises its pitch. The tone wavers and cries, as light gleams on the guitar. He stumbles through a galloping rhythm and clumsily grabs a power cord, which buzzes until it fades into the clatter of beer bottles and the whispers of would be lovers.

David steps down from the edge of the stage, wipes the sweat from his forehead with the back of his hand, and stands for a moment to allow his eyes to recover from the intense stage lighting. When they have adjusted, he walks along the edge of the stage toward the backstage door. He pushes the door open and steps through to meet a blockade. The other members of *The Swifts* stand together to confront him. His heart thumps against his sternum, and blood rushes into his arms and face as though he were preparing to battle the Hydra.

He glances from face to face. Dan Thomas, balding drummer, looks at the floor and rubs the back of his neck. Chuck Davis, bass player, yawns and scratches his belly. David realizes this is a rather lethargic Hydra. This beast has but one threat, and it is the singer, Stan Phillips, who stands squarely opposite him.

David looks up into Stan's deeply-recessed eyes, and his body tightens. He draws a spastic breath through his teeth, as Stan pulls his long red hair behind his head with both hands, holds it there for a moment to show his arm muscles, and lets it fall. David is familiar with Stan's arrogant poses and knows this one is intended to intimidate.

"What's goin' on?" David's lips twitch.

"We have to talk." Stan takes David's shoulder, holding him at arm's length.

David squirms a bit beneath Stan's hand but submits to the unwelcome contact. Maybe I'm overreacting. Maybe there is no threat here. He takes a deep breath and tries to relax, but his mind is fixed on Stan's hand, and he feels himself withering beneath the weight of it. He runs a hand through his swooping blonde hair. "What's up?"

"We've been talking."

"Who?"

"Who do you think?" Stan scowls. "You're out."

David's heart flutters. "What? What do you mean?"

"You're out of the band." Stan stares.

"Who says?"

"I do."

"But." David turns to Dan.

"Don't look at him." Stan steps closer and looks down on him. "I'm the one. I'm throwing you out. I'm sick of you fucking up our vibe with your stupid-ass hair and whining solos."

David's vision narrows to Stan's crooked smile. He sees his overlapping, coffee-stained teeth against his narrow lips with a bit of foamy, white saliva resting in the corner. David's heart throbs quickly in his chest. Heat rushes into his arms, which tremble with fierce energy.

Stan continues his onslaught, but David, staring into Stan's mouth, hears only muffled sounds.

"I mean, where do you get that stuff?" Stan moans and groans, mocking David's show-ending solo.

David watches Stan's mouth twist and contort and sees his teeth as jagged, bloody shards, and his hands curl into fists.

"Come on, asshole. You want some?" Stan beckons with raised hands.

David suddenly becomes aware of Dan and Chuck, standing by Stan, and his chin quivers.

"You're pathetic."

David turns away and steps toward the door. As he does, he feels them watching and waiting for him to break. Pressure builds in his throat and behind his eyes, and the first tear falls. He shoves the guitar into its case, pushes through the backstage door, and walks toward the exit. Stan's laughter follows him out the back door into the alley.

In the darkness of the alley, in the misty rain and cool fall air, David sobs. His chest heaves, as he gasps and slobbers. His fitful breath rises as a foggy prayer in the distant streetlamp light.

From the darkness, a black-haired, blue-eyed woman strides into the circle of illumination beneath the streetlamp. She stands for a moment to watch him shake and cry. She raises her fists above her head and screams. The furious exclamation penetrates his body to vibrate the bones, and soothing energy flows through him to clarify his mind and calm him. David smiles, and the woman walks away, disappearing into the darkness.

David carries the guitar case to his car, puts it in the back seat, and gets in. The Honda stirs to life. Headlights beam down the alley, and David turns onto Broadway, heading toward his apartment in Old Louisville.

He parks on First Street in front of the red brick Victorian and humps his gear up two flights of stairs to the apartment his father rents for him. He showers, packs a backpack for his morning flight to New Orleans, and goes to bed.

WEDNESDAY

The stewardess calls for David's row to board. He grabs his pack, walks down the ramp onto the plane, and takes his seat. He spots a busty brunette, sitting across the aisle and eating chips one by one. When she notices him watching, she leans the open bag toward him.

"No. Thanks."

"Annabelle." She extends her hand.

"David." They share a greasy handshake.

"You a student, David?"

"Yeah. And guitarist for *The Swifts.*" He searches her eyes for signs of recognition or admiration but finds none.

"Well, I was. I left the band." He shrugs. "Just not for me. Stunted aesthetics. Artistic differences. All that." David glances at her crumb-coated cleavage.

"I see." Annabelle giggles.

They settle into their seats. David watches her buckle her seatbelt and sees her soft flesh bulge ever so slightly at the edge it. His mouth waters, and he swallows hard.

The plane hurtles down the runway to press the passengers back in their seats. Soft tissues jiggle, skeletons shake, and teeth rattle. David watches Annabelle's breasts bounce and stir in her low-cut blouse. He wants to reach out and cup them in his hand to feel their heft and to lick the salty crumbs from her swollen nipples. He imagines lying on her to wallow between her legs and how he would run his hands across her bottom and suck her plump cheek.

The plane banks south then settles.

"What ya gonna do in New Orleans?" She studies David's swooping hair and pulls a sandwich from her bag. "Visit family?"

David chews his nails and glances again at her ample cleavage. "Yeah. Thanksgivin' with dad." He swallows. "And mom."

Annabelle pops a chip into her mouth and chews it. "Y'all get along?"

He raises an eyebrow.

"I mean - well enough?"

"I've got no problem with my dad." He reaches across the aisle for a chip. "Mom, well, she's somethin' else."

"How so?"

"I don't know. She's a mess."

David closes his eyes and rubs his forehead.

"Don't wanna talk about her?"

"Maybe not."

"Okay." She bites into another chip.

Tension builds in David's shoulders, and his arms begin to tingle. He rubs the tips of his fingers together. She's a stranger. What damage could it do to talk to her? He looks at her, eating chips. "She's a slut."

Annabelle looks at him for a moment. "Your mother?"

"Yeah."

"Like cheating?"

"Yeah." He swallows. "She'll lift her skirt for any swingin' dick."

"Does your father know?"

"Yeah. He tolerates it. Meanwhile, all the neighbors laugh at him. He's just too weak to leave her. Doesn't want to be alone, I guess."

"Could be." Annabelle nibbles.

"I can't stand her."

"I can see why. The way she treats-"

"She's got this grating voice." David makes a scratchy, high-pitched drone. "And she's so prissy. Acts so proper. Like she's queen of the Goddamn neighborhood."

"Phony baloney?"

"And she's convinced that I'm gay."

"Are you?"

"No."

"I didn't think so." Annabelle smiles.

"She just can't get it outta her mind. Like the last time I saw her. Three years ago. I went home for Thanksgivin'. She just kept prying. 'Are you seeing any girls? Anyone special? Does she have big boobs?'"

Annabelle, nearly choking on her sandwich, coughs. "Are you serious?"

"Oh, yeah." David shakes his head. "I guess she likes 'em."

"Wow." Annabelle hands David a sandwich. "You like ham?"

"Of course." Both smile.

"She just kept prying, asking questions about stuff that's none of her business. I mean, maybe if we had a relationship. But we don't, so every question was like she's trying to pull the teeth right outta my mouth. I clammed up. Then she hit me with the big one: 'When am I gonna have a grandchild?'"

"Doesn't she care about school?"

"No. Just a grandchild. That's all she wants. But I'm not interested. So, she got it in her head that I'm gay. And she'd be damned if she was going to eat Thanksgivin' dinner with a faggot. She started yelling about her gay son, sent the turkey flying across the kitchen, and called her idiot mother and the police. Then, before the police arrived, she came at me with a hairbrush, swinging it like a banshee. I just covered my head while she hacked at me with the bristles. Then she strutted down the hall, yelling, 'Get your shoes on, boy. You're goin' to jail.'"

"I met the police at the door and was trying to explain the situation, when she stormed in. She's all, 'get this faggot outta my house.' Then her mother came in the back, 'what are you doing to my baby?' Good God, I couldn't take any more. I just lost it. I broke down crying. My whole life, these idiots have made me miserable, so I crawled under a desk and broke. Just broke."

"When the lady officer reached under the desk to pull me out, I took her hand and put it on my cheek. I don't know. I just needed a bit of care. Anyway, she put a wrist lock on me. Mother insisted that the officers remove me from her house. Aint seen or spoken to her since."

Annabelle shows David a sad face.

"I'm sorry you have to deal with her, David." Annabelle finishes her sandwich and reaches into her bag for dessert.

David relaxes deeply into his seat, closes his eyes, and falls asleep.

When he wakes, he sees Annabelle asleep and takes the opportunity to really study her. Her almond-shaped face features high cheek bones, a small chin and nose, and full, pouty lips. Her thin eyebrows arch gracefully, showing interest even while she sleeps, and her slender neck curves delicately into her shoulders. He stretches his neck a bit to watch her breasts press against her shirt when she breathes and feels himself grow aroused.

Someone behind him coughs, and David, feeling observed and judged as a pervert, looks away from the sleeping beauty. He turns on the overhead light and, pulls a pulp magazine from his backpack, and opens it to read a couple poems.

3:43 P.M. 16 December 2013

A.B. Stephens

A long shadow stretches across a snowman stump,
my mind unravels the grimy strands of work,
and I wait in my truck for my child to run to me.

Young woman I glimpse and dream
as curls bounce black, and porn flash eye lashes bat,
perchance we'll meet and frolic in the sunshine of this day.

Our eyes lock, and I feel pathetic and ashamed,
a leering, balding husband, father, and man.

Heartache

A.B. Stephens

I've got jagged shards of iron
in the chambers of my soul,
and you, my dear, are a magnet
pull, pull, pulling upon them,
like the moon upon the sea,
until my longing grows a bit too strong,
and I drift in the wake of your loveliness.

David closes his eyes to relish the image of a man swept off his feet and floating after a divine woman. A painting comes to his mind to lend color and composition to the scene. He sees the image clearly but can't recall the artist's name. Is it Gustav Klimt? Paul Klee? Marc Chagall?

He drifts into a stream of images, following one to the next as they shift and combine. He enters the realm of imagination completely, and the remainder of the flight passes without notice until the plane swoops into the airport. The tires impact the runway, the reverse thrusters roar, and David wakes.

"We're here." Annabelle pushes the hair from her face.

"Maybe we can get together."

"Sure." Annabelle smiles.

As they exchange numbers and prepare to exit the plane, Annabelle says she hopes everything goes well with his mother. She leans into him for a hug. He smells the chips on her and feels her round softness press against him. He knows she can feel his excitement and inwardly thanks God or whoever for her presence on the flight.

David and his father shake hands at the arrival gate, and the two walk to his father's old truck. They chat about the flight, the weather, and school. His father says they are going to stop by the house to say hello to mother before going on to the hotel. David groans, as his heart sinks.

The prospect of spending time with her, pretending he has been a nurturing parent, makes David feel sick. If only his father would understand, then maybe he wouldn't drive him down this too familiar street.

"Be civil with her. She loves you in her way."

"It's a strange way."

"People are funny." Father chuckles. "And your mother is the funniest person I know."

Every landmark, every click of the odometer brings more tension into David's wiry body, and a pain grows steadily at the base of his skull, as they enter the neighborhood. David imagines jumping from the truck and running into the woods behind the neighborhood. As a youngster he would go into those woods to escape her when she raged. David sits motionless, watching raindrops splatter on the windshield. He stares into the droplets and sees her there, reflected countless times, forming a hateful chorus, which chants, "Outta my house, fucking faggot."

The truck sways from side to side like a boat on rough water. The air grows thick and moist, and beads of sweat glisten on David's forehead. Hitting a large pothole, the truck rears and bucks, and sweat runs down David's tense cheeks to drip off his chin. He shifts his focus to see, beyond the rain-spattered windshield, his childhood home, a single-story grey stucco house beneath a dark cloud. His stomach churns, his nerves tingle, and his heart beats wildly. The house grows large in the windshield, and he imagines her hateful eyes hovering over him, ever-vigilant for signs of abnormality. He feels the oppressive weight of that all-consuming emotional black hole and holds his breath, wriggles his feet, squirms in his seat. The cab of the truck presses in on him, and he stares out the window for relief. He sees only Mother's cramped, cloud-bound, grey abode.

David's father shakes his leg, "Let's do it." He laughs.

He looks at his father, studies the deep laugh lines at the corners of his eyes and on his forehead. He thinks about the embarrassment and humiliation of being married to that slutty bitch. How has he endured the repeated betrayal and disrespect? David had always assumed it was cowardice or inertia that kept his father with her. Now, looking at him compassionately, David sees his good-natured humility and realizes it is not weakness but a heroic capacity to suffer that allows his father to endure her corrupt infidelity and still find genuine joy in life. David chokes back a tear. He wants to embrace his father to take his strength and understanding into himself but merely nods his assent.

He stretches his legs and swings opens the truck door. They walk to the back of the house, where David reaches reluctantly for the doorknob. The door swings open. His eyes grow large, and his fists shake. Time stops, and David sees, there to greet him, his wild-eyed mother: flaming red hair teased into a giant war bonnet, teeth glinting as she snarls, raging at the air with a stiff-bristled hair brush.

The vision passes. His heart settles, and he steps inside to find she is not home.

Colonel Kurtz has left the compound. David breathes a sigh of relief and asks his father to take him to the hotel.

When David inquires about local events, the hotel's concierge tells him Jacques Laffont, an amazing gypsy jazz guitarist, is playing at The Old Absinthe House. He decides to attend the show. He wants to get high first, so he walks in the rain to Saint Louis Cemetery.

The sky is countless shades of grey, and what light there is seems to come from everywhere. David feels he is walking through a dreamscape and half expects to meet Marie Lafoe amongst the crypts. Instead, he finds a teenage boy with pot to spare.

The joint smolders and smokes with the scent of the swamp, and David inhales deeply. He holds the smoke in his lungs as long as possible. Soon his vision becomes clear, and he becomes aware of the warmth and substance of his body. He sits on the edge of the bed, feeling the mattress give as he breathes. His right shoulder feels tight. David slowly windmills his arm through the air, and the shoulder loosens.

He pulls the magazine from his pocket and turns to the next piece.

She

Stephen Alexander

In a shining silver display, a burlesque ballerina spins and
struts across an
angry American stage.
"Come down from your cross,
renouncer of flesh.
Do I not please you?"
"Get behind me temptress."
"Temptress? What in me tempts you?
Rather what in you responds
to the sight of me?
Is it not your desire that you condemn?
And why? Is it not the better part of you?
Reason leads you astray. Fine words deceive,
but your heart knows
what is right and proper,
despite what those with power say.
Ignore the self-hating parade pissers
and holy rollers,
who slay the dragon of instinct so sweet.
Turn away from the criminal cowards
who slur 'sinner'
at the sight of a happy person.
Free yourself from the tyranny
of robed inquisitors and money-grubbing,
snake-handling, leering fools.
Take up the bourdon of free will without fear of fiery fictions
and American Taliban.
Break the velvet ropes of solemnity and live."

David closes the magazine, smiles, and gets up from the bed to check himself in the mirror.

Hair ruffled? Check.

Bangs swooping? Check.

Eyes glistening? Check.

Expression scowling? Just enough.

Teeth shining? We can't all be perfect.

Satisfied, David begins the short walk to The Absinthe at the corner of Rue Bourbon and Rue Bienville.

He sways slowly past the voodoo and tee shirt shops and recalls Mardi gras girls giggling and cooing as they thrill the boys with their bare breasts, bouncing beneath strings of beads. He stops in a bar and orders a Hurricane, downs the drink, and heads back onto the street. His face flushes and he feels his arms and legs jiggle a little as he walks and looks up at the wrought iron balconies with their flower gardens glowing in the street lights. He feels the street embrace him and welcome him into her comforting expanse. This is his home no matter where he keeps his bed. This street welcomes him like a mother should.

Approaching The Absinthe, David sees the crowd of patrons standing on the sidewalk to peer into the bar with the hope of glimpsing Jacques. A twisting violin melody captures his attention and pulls him into the gently-swaying crowd. He makes his way to the bar and orders a Hurricane and grooves to the rhythms of the group.

Even without the marque front man, the group enthralls. David's toes tap and his head bobs, as the guitars and base fiddle pump out insistent beats. The violin player cuts loose with a long, bouncing tone that nearly topples David, who staggers like a drunken sailor on rough seas. He receives his Hurricane, takes a long drink of the cold, reddish concoction from the disposable plastic glass, as the tones fill his ears and a smile spreads across his face.

Struggling to raise his empty glass into the air, he orders another.

The violin plays the skipping melody to *Minor Swing*, and the base fiddle thumps its response. They repeat the intro. Again they play the hypnotic passage. Anticipation grows, the atmosphere electrifies, and everyone in the audience looks wide-eyed toward the stage. David sees only the twinkling stage lights beyond heads and shoulders. The low murmur, which fills the hall, erupts into wild cheers, as Jacques staggers onto the stage. David drinks, the violin repeats the intro, and everyone bounces and sways. David's hair stands on end, as Jacques knocks out a few ethereal chords, and a surge of energy slows through David's body. The guy has magic, or at least showmanship.

Jacques plays a meandering, popping run with such inflection and intonation that David feels every nuance. The guitar sings and cries. David's chin quivers, as the music soaks into his soul. The violin soars above the whole grinding, chopping clockworks with a seeming disregard for time, and his heart flutters. The song ends, and the crowd cheers.

David closes his eyes and drifts into a fantasy in which he walks alone down a dark alley. His foggy breath drifts and glows in the distant streetlamp light. A thin layer of rain water coats the brick-paved alley to make the road to sparkle like the night sky underfoot. Pressure builds at the back of his neck and David knows someone is following him. Hard heels clack on the pavement, and the sound echoes off the brick walls to create an ominous soundscape.

Too frightened to look back, David stares toward an arched gate at the end of the alley and hastens toward it, as Jacques begins playing the haunting *Si Tu Savais*.

A raven-haired gypsy woman walks slowly into the light at the end of the alley. Her flowing red skirt sways, as she takes long, lunging steps and bounces slowly with Jacques' rhythm. She wraps her red shawl tightly around her torso, and its loose ends drape on her round bottom and wrinkle left and right as she struts.

She twirls and throws her arms into the air to reveal her narrow waist and the contrasting curves of her breasts. David is caught up in the drama of the dance. He claps with the beat. The dancer holds her skirt out above her head and shimmies left and right like a butterfly in flight. Her skirt flutters with the music to reveal briefly her smooth, shapely legs, shining in the light from the street lamp. Her hair sways. Her dress flows. Her breasts bounce. The twirling blur of color and sensuality enthralls David, and he feels the tingling pressure, as he grows thick and strong.

The music and the dance run out of time, and she falls to the pavement. One final note sounds briefly, then David opens his eyes. I must see this guy, this Jacques Laffont.

He pushes into the crowd, nudges past the other revelers along the length of the brass-trimmed bar, toward the stage. Approaching the densely-packed front of the crowd, his body tingles, and his head throbs. He peers over a few shoulders but still can't see Jacques. He pushes forward toward the stage and feels the crush of the crowd. Every part of his body is poked with an elbow, pressed with a hip, smothered with a belly, brushed with a breast, or breathed upon.

The air is sticky hot and smells vaguely fruity with the scent of so many different drinks exhaled from so many mouths. Amid the alcoholic pot pori, David can smell the rich, caramel breath of the bourbon drinker next to him. The man turns to him, smiles, and runs a hand through his own swooping blonde hair.

"Man, this guy is somethin' else."

David leans left but sees only the backs of heads and shoulders.

"And that guitar." The man shakes his head in disbelief. "Ya gotta see that thing."

Jacques plays *Isn't She Lovely* with such passion and ferocity that the notes blend together in a blur of ephemeral sounds that defy comprehension. David's heart soars, and his body thrills. He rises up on his toes but still sees only heads and shoulders.

"It has presence." The bourbon drinker slurs and pops. "It's alive."

The revelers at the very front jostle and shift, and an opening toward the stage appears. David peers through it, and a bright light stuns his eyes. He stares into the light, and gradually his eyes adjust. As he stares deeper into the light, he sees Jacques Laffont. David shoots the bourbon drinker an astonished look. He can't believe what he sees.

Jacques Laffont resembles a poorly-controlled skeleton marionette with a two-day beard and greasy black hair hanging in his eyes. Skinny arms dangle and jerk from bulbous elbows. Bony fingers scrape and scratch at the strings, and his tiny neck juts from slumping shoulders, as his balding head dangles over the guitar.

How can this thing make such beautiful music?

Laffont plays. He ignores the crowd and plays until, in the middle of the song, he breaks into *Come as You Are* and lifts his head slightly. Blotchy, purplish-grey skin stretches taut and twitches across his skull. He parts his papery eyelids with visible effort and looks with bulging eyes directly at David, who meets his gaze.

A high-pitched tone grows in David's mind. It's as though his very bones vibrate at a constant rate to produce the alarming tone from the depths of his body. The tone grows louder to dominate his consciousness with its unwavering drone.

David's eyelids flutter, and all traces of thought disappear from his mind, as his consciousness fills with the perception of Jacques and his blonde Manouche guitar, shining golden like the sun in the stage lights. Her immodestly undulating curves and wild range of tones bespeak sensuality beyond the mundane, beyond all normal sex, beyond all perversion. Her presence is something more. It is transcendent. It is sacred.

David watches Jacques caress her in his lap, strumming her taut strings. His blood boils, his muscles tighten, and his hands curl into fists. Anger twists his face into a primitive mask, and molten envy is cast into the mold of dark intention.

David's head spins, as the tone ringing in his ears twists into his brain like a drill bit. As the pain intensifies, he looks around to see on every face a strange expression. He feels looked upon, observed, and accused. Heat radiates through his body, and sweat soaks his clothes. He tries to stand still and breathe steadily, but his stomach convulses, and he gasps. He runs a hand across his forehead and looks at it, glowing red in the stage light.

"You all right, buddy?" The scent of bourbon sticks to David's face.

He stares at the man. His heart pounds in his chest and throbs in his temples.

"Let's get you outta here."

The bourbon drinker pushes through the crowd to lead David toward the exit. David feels people knock against him with their knees and elbows. Dizziness descends on him, and his head rolls on his shoulders. The strength fades from his legs, and he struggles to stay on his feet, to keep walking, to get away from this hostile crowd.

"Come on, buddy."

They arrive at the sidewalk, and the bourbon drinker leads him around the corner, through the arched gate, and into the garden next to the Absinthe. David leans against the building, as saliva fills his mouth and flows through his parted lips. His whole experience is reduced to the growing expectation of the convulsions and the splatter. His stomach churns and his face goes pale and cold. His stomach muscles contract, and vomit spews from his mouth and splashes against the building. The fluorescent yellow fluid runs down the beige wall, and thick chunks hang in the stucco. Another spastic convulsion folds him over, and a gurgling mixture of air and bile spews from his mouth and splatters his shoes and pant legs.

David leans against the building. His heart settles until his pulse and breathing return to normal, and his face flushes deep red. He groans, as he rubs the back of his hand against his mouth and spits out the last of the revoltingly-bitter vomit.

The bourbon drinker presses something into David's hand.

"Hold this."

The side door to the Absinthe swings open, and light from the doorway spills into the garden to flow across the shrubs and flowers. David hides and watches. His vision narrows to the silhouette of a man holding a guitar case in the doorway. The man steps through the doorway into the garden. David's eyes grow large, and a sick smile spreads across his face when he recognizes the man. It is Jacques Laffont. He lurks in the darkness and watches the gypsy struggle to set the guitar case on top of the garbage can. As the guitarist relieves himself, David feels something heavy in his right hand and, looking down, realizes it is a brick. He shakes it in his hand a few times to study its mass. Then, gripping it firmly, David glares at the guitarist. His heartbeat turns jazzy, and breath hisses at the back of his open mouth.

David creeps toward Jacques. Step after stealthy step, David closes in on the oblivious Laffont. His toe scuffs across a protruding brick, and Jacques twists his scrawny neck to look across his shoulder. David stands as still as he can, wavering only slightly. Jacques returns his gaze to the ground before him.

David continues his stalking approach. He feels his heart beat in his arms and face, and his steamy breath quickens, as he arrives behind the decrepit musician. The acidic smell of Laffont's urine burns David's eyes and nose, and just as his eyes begin to water, his cell phone rings.

Jacques turns.

He looks into David's desperate eyes and, recognizing the situation, smiles to show his crooked, yellow teeth.

David lifts the brick high above his shoulder. He catches sight of his reflection in Laffont's bulging, exhausted eyes but can't quite comprehend what he sees there. He doesn't recognize the reality of the situation, as his torso lunges toward Jacques, and his arm swings down.

He swings the brick at Laffont's head, catches him with a glancing blow that gouges through the skin of his right cheek. A flap of skin hangs loosely, glistening with blood. David strikes again, smashing Jacques' forehead with the brick. His head snaps back and his body jerks, as the force of the blow rattles through every joint of his frail body. Jacques falls to his knees on the brick patio, and blood runs down his nose to drip into the puddle of urine.

Laffont kneels passively. David growls and delivers the killing blow to the crown of his head. The corner of the brick crunches into Laffont's skull, and shards of bone and chunks of flesh sail through the air to splatter the door, the wall, and David.

Laffont's face droops, and his mouth falls open. His body collapses in a heap.

David drops to his knees and pounds Laffont's head. Sloppy splashing sounds, punctuated by crushing thuds, fill the garden.

Shaking and blood-spattered, David clambers to his feet. He stares blankly at what was recently a man but now resembles a pile of dirty clothes lying on a floor. His chest heaves, as he breathes heavily. He looks at the man's crushed skull and sees blood, flowing from the gaping hole to mix with the urine. As he stares, the bloody cocktail oozes toward his feet.

"Dude, you gotta get outta here." The bourbon drinker pushes David's shoulder.

David drops the bloody brick, which twists slowly as it falls. A tuft of hair flutters from the corner of the brick, as it clacks, scuttles, and scrapes against the patio.

Leaning his head slightly, David looks at the man. "What nice hair you have."

David takes the guitar case in his hand, glances over his shoulder, and walks in a daze to the back of the garden. He stands still for a long moment to look left and right then walks to the right through the interconnected gardens.

The streets of the French Quarter are never empty, but at the moment only a few bleary-eyed drunks walk near him. David keeps his head low and walks swiftly toward the hotel. He holds the case with both hands. His body bends at the waist, as he struggles to support the surprisingly heavy guitar case.

"David. David, is that you?"

Approaching his hotel, he slows briefly but keeps his head turned.

"It's Annabelle. From the airplane." She trots toward him and waves.

He quickly enters the front doors of his hotel and makes his way to his room.

David sits, shakes, and stares.

The dark silhouette of the guitar case keeps vigil, as he stares into the distance, beyond the wall of his room, back to the garden beside The Absinthe.

Blood-spattered memories jerk and twitch through his body.

A bloody brick turns slowly in the air. "Hold this." Blood splatters. A tuft of black hair flutters.

THURSDAY

Police sirens accompany dawn, and their flashing lights play on his curtains, as the cars pass.

David sits, shakes, and stares.

The dark silhouette of the guitar case keeps vigil, as he stares into the distance, beyond the wall of his room, back to the garden beside the Absinthe.

Blood-spattered memories jerk and twitch through his body.

FRIDAY

Dawn breaks. Light spreads through the window across the unused bed to the chair with the guitar case perched upon it and finds David, looking about with a two-day beard and greasy hair hanging in his eyes.

Warm water flows from the shower over David's head and shoulders. Blood flows down the drain. His body relaxes, and he recalls that he has killed Jacques Laffont. His body relives the event. It feels the forces and movements of his assault, and he recalls the blood, flowing down the guitarist's nose past his staring eyes. I have killed Jacques Laffont. David rubs his hands together to wash away the last of the blood. There's nothing I can do about that. He washes his face. I don't know about justice. Contrition is a private matter. Confession is between a man and God. And retribution is best left to fate. Dirty water swirls down the drain.

Clean and wearing only a robe, David puts the bloody clothes and shoes into the black garbage bag from the can in his room. He ties the bag and walks to the door. He reaches for the knob, and someone knocks. He freezes, and his heart jumps to his throat. Another set of three knocks. David stands as a living monument to guilt; pupils dilated, eyes cast sideways, brows raised, jaw hanging.

A female voice floats through the door.

"Open up."

Barely breathing, David stares at the door. The capillaries in his eyes swell with blood, and veins pop up on his temples.

"Open up. I know you're in there."

David looks to the window, considering an escape.

"I saw what you did, David." The voice whispers.

His heart pounds. Pain spreads through his head, as he leans his ear against the door.

"I won't tell anyone," she whispers, "but you must open the door."

Sweat runs down his cheeks, as he reaches slowly for the knob.

"That's it, honey. Just open the door."

David wraps his shaking hand around the knob and swallows hard, as he slowly unlocks the door.

"You have nothing to fear."

He turns the knob and opens the door to see, standing in the hall, radiant beneath the flickering hallway light, a beautiful black-haired woman, wearing a flowing red dress and heels. David's body tingles when he recognizes her. It is the woman who danced in his dream. She is the same woman who screamed beneath the streetlamp.

She stands before him with his darkest secret in hand.

He looks into her ice-blue eyes and feels a deep, complicated longing for her. He wants to fall into her arms and languish there against her breasts. He wants to cry in her embrace. He wants to bathe her in his tears. He reaches out to her, and she gives him her hand. When he touches her, and a jolt of emotion flows through his body to electrify his fingertips. Tears flow from his eyes, and he collapses into her arms. They step into the room, and she closes the door.

She leads him, wobbling, to the bed, where they collapse. He rolls his head onto her shoulder and weeps quietly. She consoles him with a gentle hand, pulling his face deeper into her silky, vanilla-scented, black hair. The sweet scent envelops him, fills his lungs and veins and soul with dark, sticky desire, and he knows he has found what he has unknowingly sought.

"Justine."

She strokes the nape of his neck and lifts her head up so that her red lips brush his ear. She whispers gently. It's little more than a soft breath swirling through his ear into the secret depths of his mind. David nods, and a chill travels his spine, as his body sinks into the mattress. His mind becomes still and bright, and his whole being smiles. Content and at one with the world, he closes his eyes, while she pulls the robe from his shoulders.

SATURDAY

Soft morning light winnows through the lacy curtains and flows across his naked body, which shines in the dimly-lit room. Slowly, David's eyelids lift, and his mind withdraws from dreams of Justine and the guitar. He knows without reaching out or looking that she isn't there, but, before him, the black guitar case awaits his attention.

He walks the few steps to the chair, picks up the case, and sets it flat on the bed. He opens the buckles one by one and excitedly cracks open the lid. His heart races, and his face lights up like a young child tearing into a brightly-wrapped Christmas present. He makes a small sound, almost a squeal, expressing pure selfish joy unmixed with guilt or remorse.

He throws back the lid and looks inside. When he sees what is there, he gasps and pulls his hands to his chest. His eyes open wide, and the blood runs from his face. A chill sets in at the base of his spine and spreads through his torso like frost across a window.

The guitar is decrepit.

It looks as though it has been ignored for decades. Several of the strings are broken, the neck is bowed, the fret board is warped, the sound chamber is lined with a fine powder of disintegrated wood, the finish is crackled, and the top is cracked.

David holds his hands to his face. Is this the same guitar? Did I kill Jacques Laffont for this rotten corpse? He throws the lid over the guitar and squeezes his eyes tightly shut. Heat rushes through his body to dissolve the ice that had formed there. His face tingles as blood floods into the capillaries, and he hears an electric guitar wail. Tension stiffens his shoulders and neck until he feels like a scarecrow.

Someone knocks at the door.

"David, honey. It's Mother."

Rage grows in him like cancer in a lab rat. He feels it pressing against his organs to squeeze his spleen and pinch his nerves.

"Why didn't you come to Thanksgiving?"

He feels himself grow ugly, as the cancerous rage pressurizes his body and twists his face.

"How could you do this to dear ol' mom?"

He bolts to the door and throws it open to see her, all made up with a caring face brushed on over her scowl. He steps through the doorway and stares, stone-faced, at the stranger whom he had called mother.

At the sight of him, Mother's façade crumbles, and a new expression reveals itself. Her lips jerk back at the corners. Her eyebrows bob up and down briefly before settling akimbo.

"What do you want?" He leans close to her.

"Uh. Uh." She casts her gaze to the side.

"Well. What do you want from me?"

"You missed-" She swallows hard. "You missed Thanksgiving."

"Yet you managed without me." David smiles. "And I did fine without you."

"Listen to me, David Rene." Mother pecks the air with her finger.

"No. You listen to me." David barely raises his voice. "I don't need you."

"I am your mother." She cackles.

"There was a time when I needed you, but you shit on me and called me names."

Her mouth hangs open, as he continues in an even voice.

"Now I am supposed to crawl back to your table? Continue begging for scraps of affection? Pay you tribute by calling you mother? Well, you've never been a mother to me, and I will not come to your table again."

She stares blankly.

"Now leave me alone." He closes the door.

Realizing it is Saturday and his flight leaves in a few hours, David smokes the last of his weed and flushes the roach. He packs his backpack and throws it on his shoulder. He picks up the guitar case in one hand and the garbage bag filled with bloody clothes in the other. He looks around the room one last time and lets his eyes linger on the bed, where he had melted into Justine's embrace.

David opens the door and steps into the hall, careful to avoid the doorjamb with the bulky guitar case. He walks down the red and cream carpeted hall until he comes to the housekeeper's cart. He stuffs the black bag into the garbage bin with those from the other rooms and continues to the checkout desk.

"How was your stay?"

"Fine. Thanks."

"I just need you to sign here."

David signs the form and picks up the case. As he turns to leave, two officers approach.

"Mr. Guiot?"

"Yes." David's heart races.

"We'd like a word."

The guitar becomes incredibly heavy in his hand. He wants to set it down, but one of the officers gently guides him a few steps from the desk for privacy. Now they stand at the end of the hall, just a few feet away from the maid's cart. David pants. His free hand shakes, so he thrusts it into the pocket of his jeans.

"Are you alright, David?"

"Yes." He answers immediately. How do they know my name? "What's this about?"

"Your mother called." The officer looks deeply into his eyes, and David feels the officer's stiff, accusing presence in his soul.

"What?"

"Your mother. She's worried about you. I'm starting to wonder myself."

"I'm fine. I'm fine. Just-"

"Just what?"

"I'm nervous, I guess."

"A little high maybe?"

"Yeah."

"You a musician, David?"

He notices he is swinging the guitar case back and forth and holds it still.

"David. Do you play?"

"Yes."

"D'ja hear 'bout what happened the other night? Jacques Laffont?"

"Who?" He steps aside to allow the cleaning woman to push her cart past.

"Never mind. Can I see your guitar?"

"My guitar?"

"Yes, sir, the one in your hand." The officers smile at each other.

"Oh. Okay." David hands the guitar case to him.

The officer sets the case on a table and unsnaps the buckles one at a time. David hears every nuance of each one opening. He breathes heavily and feels the blood flow through his arms. His body burns with fear, and sweat drips from his face, as the officer pulls back the top of the case and looks inside. He stares into it for a moment then turns his gaze toward David and laughs.

"Can't nobody play this thang."

They all burst out laughing, David especially. He laughs loudly, as the tension in his body transforms into unadorned, staccato cackling. Tears well up in his eyes, and joy sweeps through his body until he feels he is about to float off his feet.

"David." The officer stares beneath heavy eyebrows. "David." He takes him by the elbow. "How 'bout you take your guitar back to your room for a couple hours. We want you to be safe on the streets."

"But I just checked out."

"It'll be okay. I'll say somethin' to the desk clerk, and, David," he smiles, "be nice to your mother. She's the only one you'll ever have."

Back in Louisville, David opens the guitar case. He looks inside, and his heart aches. Tears well up in his eyes. His hands shake, and his breath catches in his throat, as he takes the decrepit guitar from its case. A storm of discordant sounds pours from the guitar, as the loose ends of broken strings swing about. Holding the guitar at arm's length, he takes in the pitiful sight. Lowering the guitar to his lap, he gasps and chokes back a sob. After a moment, he takes a soft cotton cloth and rubs her top. The finish becomes shiny smooth and reddish. He continues rubbing, and she begins to shine, almost glow, with renewed vitality.

David strokes the back of her neck, and his eyes pop open wide, as the neck slowly straightens in his hand. He drops the guitar on his bed and jumps up. Backing away, he stares in disbelief, as broken strings flutter through the air and mend themselves. The hollow body of the guitar shrinks and changes into the familiar shape of a solid body, electric guitar, and the finish turns a lustrous red.

David cautiously approaches the transformed guitar. He reaches out a trembling hand to take her by the neck. She is solid and heavy. He strokes her sumptuously-curving sides, and music comes to his imagination. The complex, resonant passages stir deep within his psyche to send chills through his body.

He plugs the guitar into an amplifier and places his fingers on the strings. He closes his eyes, takes a deep breath, and lets it slide out between pursed lips, and his mind settles briefly into silence. Then a shockwave stirs the still air of his small apartment, as he unleashes a fierce barrage of twisting, slurring, and bewitching tones.

The music flows through his veins like heroin, and he feels a warm rush, a joyous glow, as every cell in his body slurps up the wicked tones. His heart tingles with life and longing, and he sinks into the music, into the minute silences between rapid-fire notes, into the place where future and past, here and there, mingle.

In this moment, he sees Stan walk naked through a door. In his hand, he holds a noose. He adjusts the loop and slides it over his head. He lifts his long, sparkling hair out of the way and tightens the noose around his neck. Flesh bulges, arteries swell, and Stan steps onto a low bench. He slides the rope through an eye bolt and pulls it tight. He ties the rope in a knot and lifts his left foot from the bench. Closing his eyes, he slides a hand across an ass cheek, and out of his sight the bedroom door swings open to reveal Justine, smiling.

As Stan fondles himself, she walks to him and watches. Just as he reaches full arousal, she kicks the bench from beneath his feet. His bare feet drop an inch. The noose cinches around his throat. He reaches up with his right hand to grab the rope, but he can't loosen it. He kicks wildly, and his face turns crimson. He grabs at the door frame. Fingernails scrape at and dig into the wood, but he can't hold it. His feet stop flailing, and his hands fall to his sides. His body swings slowly, steadies, and stops.

Justine smiles.

David plays for days. He doesn't eat. He doesn't bathe. He does nothing but play but still doesn't begin to exhaust the blood and music in the guitar. When exhaustion overcomes him, he falls asleep on the floor with the guitar in his lap.

TUESDAY

The door knob turns, and the door glides open. Through it, steps the radiant, blue-eyed beauty, Justine. She walks slowly toward him and stops to stand over his exhausted body. Her hair flutters in a small breeze from the window and glistens in the fading light of the setting sun. She stands in the surreal light of dusk and looks at David, sprawled out on the floor. She reaches up to the neck of her red dress. Red fingernails flash as she unbuttons the top button. She slides her hand down to the next one to pop it through the hole and continues until the dress hangs from her shoulders to reveal a slash of golden flesh.

She lets the dress fall over her breasts. It hangs from her hips briefly then falls to the floor, and she steps out of the dress to kick it toward him. She kneels next to his unconscious body, draws close to his ear, and whispers.

Standing, she looks into a large round mirror, hanging on the wall. She turns slightly left and right to study her delightful form. A slight smile forms on her face, and the substance of her body fades. A flash of blue light bursts through from within to obliterate the illusion of her physical existence. The blue light rushes toward the mirror and enters it to pass through, taking the reflective coating with it.

Later that evening, David wakes and struggles to his feet. He manages to stand crookedly. Shoulders bowed. Back bent. He looks into the mirror to find only clear glass, and a crescendo of trumpets blasts his mind. Raising his hands to cover his face, David collapses to the floor.

Charlotte

Charlotte peels her bare arm from the truck's vinyl seat and adjusts the mirror to check her face. She gazes deeply into the rectangular rearview and smiles with surprise. She still recognizes herself, still discerns her smooth, plump lips and high cheek bones despite the swollen, inky bruises. She studies her blue eyes in the mirror. Something is missing. They don't sparkle as when she was a child, or even a year ago, when she was twenty-one, and first started up with Ethan.

Leaving the apartment rental office, Ethan walks into the image on the rearview. His black flattop sparkles with sweat, and his biceps strain the sleeves of his tee shirt.

"All set." Ethan jangles a set of keys. "Let's get the bed. I'll get this end." Ethan heaves the mattress. "You catch that end. Don't drop it."

She struggles to keep up her end, which presses against her baby bump.

"Come on now. Up the steps. Let's go. Down the hall. Lay it here."

Piece by piece, they struggle up with the furniture: Box springs, clanking bed rails, old cloth couch, television, and clothes on metal hangers and in boxes. They spread their stuff out in the old-carpet living room, plastic bathroom, galley kitchen, and small bedroom, where Charlotte notices the closet door, leaning to one side. She studies the slightly diagonal lines of the door frame and notices that the rectangular door is trapped inside the trapezoidal frame. The frame pinches the door at the corners as though the building were trying to crush it. She pulls the cool brass-plated doorknob, but the door doesn't budge. She runs her hand along the frame and catches a splinter in the tip of her index finger.

Standing at the vanity, she sees the wooden barb, protruding from her finger. A drop of blood domes up on the skin around it, and throbbing pain shoots into her palm and wrist. She pulls at the splinter, and it slips from her finger. A drop of blood splashes into the sink and explodes on the plastic basin. Blood trickles toward the drain, and a tear slips from her eye.

"Come on, Baby. It's not that bad. I'll deal with that door later." He cups her breast in his hand. "Now I want to deal with you."

The sun sinks toward the horizon, and its light fades upon the increasingly blood-smeared couple.

As she kneels on the mattress for his pleasure, she stares at the crooked closet and traces its stressed outline with her eyes. Slowly, she becomes aware of a dim glow. A ghastly yellow light creeps beneath the door and across the carpet. It's a strange nighttime sunrise that spills into her miserable existence, bringing with it, as every dawn does, the implicit promise of redemption.

Charlotte stares at the door. The door stares back, winking with its mysterious light.

She dreams of walking through a meadow toward a castle, standing high upon a sun-drenched hill. The colorful autumn leaves on the trees crackle in a cool breeze, and sunlight shimmers through the leaves and across the ground. As she approaches the castle entrance, a small deer joins her to frolic and play. As she nears the castle, she sees it is made of presents wrapped in shining, colorful paper. They form a high, impenetrable wall topped with defensive crenellations. She hears laughter and singing inside, and her body tingles with joy and anticipation.

When she wakes in the darkness just before sunrise, Charlotte sits on the edge of the bed alone. She studies the light seeping beneath the closet door onto the carpet. Something about the color disturbs her. It is harsh yellow, brassy and unstable, shifting about from golden to greenish. As she watches the light, her stomach churns, her mouth fills with saliva, and beads of sweat form on her forehead. She sits with her head in her hands and fights off the urge to vomit.

She recalls kneeling on the motel floor to grovel at Ethan's feet. Like a supplicant to some horrible god, she begs not for mercy or forgiveness but that he would never leave her. His black eyes thunder down, menacing her last square inch of integrity, the last bit that will never submit. Giant hovering eyes in the sky above her fairy tale castle keep.

Sunlight flows into the room. The sickly yellow light fades, and the nausea passes.

Charlotte finds a screwdriver in a small box of tools. She wedges it between the closet door and the door jam and pries. Her arms quake with the effort. The wood pops and snaps, but the door does not budge.

Ethan pushes Charlotte aside.

"Let me do it."

He grips the handle with both hands, puts a foot up against the wall, and pulls with all his might. Veins rise up on his arms and forehead, his face glows red, and sweat drips from his nose. The door crackles its resistance, and the air escaping Ethan's throat makes a girlish squeak. Pretending not to notice, Charlotte turns away and begins to make the bed.

Ethan's fist arcs through the air to land squarely against the white door. It thumps and rattles in its frame, and light pops around the edges. Quickly, he pulls at the knob. Again. He pulls and rattles and jerks it. Huffing and puffing, Ethan pounds on the door with his palms, leaving sweaty hand prints on the white paint.

He sits on the carpet and stares at the crooked closet door. He has no desire to know what is behind it. He only wants the door to bend to his will. Charlotte brings him a glass of water, which he takes without comment.

He drinks the water and sits to ponder the problem of the door. What tool could he use to open the door? What would provide mechanical advantage? He has no substantial pry bar. No saw. He's not ready to resort to fire. He is left with brute force.

Rested, Ethan is ready for another assault. He climbs to his feet, and squares off against the door. Stepping back with his right foot, he rocks back and forth to build a rhythm. Then, as his weight moves forward, he picks up his right foot and kicks the door. His foot lands with a tremendous thud. He grabs the door knob with both hands and pulls.

The door swings open, and yellow light explodes from inside the closet to fill the room with its sickly hue. Ethan falls on his back.

Charlotte goes to him.

"You think it's funny?"

He kicks her in the stomach. She doubles over and falls to the floor.

"I'll show you funny. How's this?" He smacks her face.

Jerking the collar of her tee shirt, he pulls her across the floor, until the shirt tears. Then, he grabs her arm and drags her into the closet.

"Now stay there." Ethan forces the door closed.

Beneath a single light bulb, Charlotte curls into a ball and sobs, as cold, stale air swirls around her half-naked body to chill her.

Once her tears fade, she stands and notices that the whole closet leans and twists so that the side walls spiral toward the back wall. Even the two clothes rods arc wildly toward the rear of the closet. She also notices that every surface, even the ceiling, is covered with yellow wallpaper. The yellow is the color of an old bruise. Black blobs of various sizes and irregular, wavy stripes provide the design on the paper. Everywhere she looks, the stripes and blobs swell and recede.

Looking into the undulating depth of the closet, Charlotte feels the strength drain from her legs. She holds her arms out and stares at a spot on the back wall and tries to balance herself, as the whole closet rocks and spins without any stable axis. Lowering herself to the floor, she crawls to the rear of the closet, where she studies the curves and blobs as they interact, overlap, draw near, and jut apart. She puts her hand against the wall and smiles.

Charlotte raises her hand to scratch the wallpaper. She scratches and peels slowly at first, then more forcefully, franticly. As she does, she sees that the paper behind is the same yellow and black design. "How many layers of this hideous yellow," she wonders.

A muffled, guttural, rage-filled scream creeps into her awareness. The more paper she removes the louder and more present the scream becomes. She feels it vibrate in her bones, and her body tingles with energy. Her muscles tighten, as the scream, ever-changing, brutal, and mad for destruction, continues. Charlotte feels it in every fiber of her body. Her muscles twitch as if dancing to the primal rage it expresses, and a bit of saliva drops from her mouth.

She sits back for a moment to study her progress. The paper is thoroughly shredded in an area the size of a dinner plate. Long strips hang in curls or lay strewn about the floor. Then something presses against the paper from behind. The paper bulges then breaks, and a reflective metal fist blasts through it. The rest of the arm juts out. Charlotte and the metal hand tear at the wallpaper, and a shining metal bulge pushes through. Then it bursts out: A reflective human female.

Charlotte and the other stand face to face, reflecting one another. Charlotte smiles and reaches a hand toward her. The reflective one mirrors her movement. The two touch hands, and Charlotte steps toward her. The reflective one also steps forward, and the two merge to leave only the single reflective form.

"Char." Ethan taps the door with a butcher knife. The knife rings out metallic tings.

"I'm ready to make up." He pulls the doorknob.

"Char. I'm talking to you!" He pulls at the door again. "Push from your side, Mar."

The door flies off its hinges, and Ethan sails through the air, eyes bulging, mouth agape, riding a wave of yellow light. The warrior stands in the closet to reflect the wallpaper's stripes and blobs and Ethan's astonished expression. Charlotte shrieks. The shrill sound fills the bedroom, the apartment, and the world. She steps into the doorway. The closet spirals behind her, and yellow light pours around.

Ethan stares wide-eyed, as he attempts to scoot across the bed.

She swings the metal bar down toward him, and he rolls out of the way, onto the floor on the far side of the bed. Charlotte leaps over the bed, and the two square off.

Slashing defensively with his knife, Ethan backs away toward the hall. She stalks.

Charlotte thrusts the rod. He swings his knife to block. Metal impacts and slides on metal, and the bar slips past Ethan's face. She steps in and twirls the bar down onto Ethan's cheek to crunch the bone. His eye pops out and dangles from the optic nerve. Holding his eyeball against his cheek, Ethan falls to his knees. Blood flows between his fingers, and he swings the knife lamely.

She strikes again, smashing Ethan's forearm. He drops the knife to the floor and writhes in agony.

He props up on an elbow, and his eye bounces across his ruined face. He extends a broken and beseeching hand toward her.

"Please. Please. Forgive me."

Charlotte stands over him, glories in the gore, and shrieks.

www.ingramcontent.com/pod-product-compliance
Lightning Source LLC
Chambersburg PA
CBHW070330130626
46556CB00007B/2785